THE FRAGILE

Finn Fairlane

The FAIRLANE *Series*

THE FRAGILE

Finn Fairlane

NICK SAVAGE

4 Horsemen
Publications, Inc.

4 Horsemen Publications, Inc.
1497 Main St. Suite 169
Dunedin, FL 34698
4horsemenpublications.com
info@4horsemenpublications.com

Cover by S. Wilder
Editor 4 Horsemen Publications, Inc.

Library of Congress Control Number: 2022941321

Paperback ISBN-13: 978-1-64450-667-7
Audiobook ISBN-13: 978-1-64450-665-3
Ebook ISBN-13: 978-1-64450-666-0

DEDICATION

For all the women I've loved before, thank you for helping to make me who I am today.

And for Kris, the one woman who has never left my side, I love you more than I can ever say.

Table of Contents

CHAPTER 1

Welcome To This World

I keep having the same dreams: dreams of a better time; dreams of a time when things were simpler; when I was younger and, perhaps, stronger than I am now. They are haunting dreams from when Faith and I were new and discovering each other in every way possible. Dreams that feel more akin to memories being played back, like a movie in my mind, while I lay in slumber.

Dreams can mean many things, but I like to believe that they show us what we miss or what we wish we could change. Some dreams show us the life we could have had, the world we secretly wish we had. Maybe that's why my dreams always seem to irk me so. Perchance this life that I lead isn't what I truly wanted in my heart of hearts. But if I know this now, I have to wonder if it is too late to have everything that I desire. If that is true, then I need to find a way to the life I should have had. Perchance, the life that I have lived was the life better off left a dream. It's that unat-tainable goal that provides ambition, but ultimately leaves you where you needed to be—not where you thought you wanted to be. Maybe that's the rub and I am too late. I may be left with nothing but dreams I never realized I had.

This dream playing right now takes me back to New Year's Eve 2000: the Millennium, the big Y2K, the supposed end of it all. Most of us knew things would turn out just fine but jumped on the hype to make the most of a night meant for parties, drinking, and being with friends, the memories of years past and the good times to come. The Auld Lang Syne, so to speak.

We were at a house party somewhere in the Lincoln Park area of Chicago, either on the outskirts of the DePaul campus or just beyond. I guess the location isn't the critical detail here since my mind can't pinpoint its exact location, but there we were. It was Faith, me, and two of her friends from back home. It's been several years since that New Year's, but their names were Henry and Wanda if I correctly recall.

The funny things about dreams are the oxymoron-ic-sounding, vague specificities of them, like trying to recall a time when you were really high or stoned on something. You know the environment and approx-imate surroundings from the moment. In hindsight, though, the details are foggy, and the chronology is wrong. The dense, hazy aura surrounds the events you know you were at, but try as you may, you can't recall them as well as you'd like. The missing moments between the significant events that stick out in your mind are gone.

I know leading up to the party we were at some guy's house who lived above some family business in a three-flat on Fullerton. We were in his house, kicking each other's asses on Goldeneye 64 and smoking some most excellent weed. I remember that and taking my third hit from the joint. The next thing I knew, we were all walking west on Fullerton to finally hit up that party. All my THC-riddled mind could see was my legs. I remember thinking that what we smoked wasn't just weed, so I had to concentrate on each step and tell my brain to lift my leg, swing it forward, and repeat. I remember the laughter from next to me as Henry, Wanda, and Faith were all entertained at my inability to walk like a capable human being. Weed had never done that to me before or since. The next thing I remember was that we were at the New Year's Eve party. That's what I mean, though—vague specificity. There are distinct moments surrounded by the nothingness of time lost during that night.

The party looked good, at least from the outside approach; way too many people huddled together on the wood-planked balcony overlooking the alley behind the building. All of them puffing away on cigarettes while keeping warm in the crisp, early winter air. Once again, we found ourselves walking up to the second story of the dark grey brick, three-flat apartment—a most common sight in the Windy City. After paying the five-dollar cover charge for the Red Solo® cup and unlimited refills of whatever was left of the second-rate beer they bought by the keg, we stepped inside the building.

As all memories of parties go, whether high or sober, the faces of anyone that doesn't end up playing a vital role in the night's memory are faceless. Not faceless, like the children from Pink Floyd's *The Wall*, but anonymous, like blurred background extras from an eighties high-school movie party scene. Generic. I am sure this party had their fair share of husky, pseu-do-intellectual young men trying to wax existential about the meaning of life and the pointlessness of it all, while their only real goal herewas a feeble attempt to nail whatever girl (or guy) they were philosophizing with. Luckily, those guys aren't the point of this dream.

After the time lapses from walking through a crowd, the next thing I remember was the bedroom. The walls were decorated with framed prints of Kant, Nietzsche, Chomsky, and other philosophers. This bedroom probably belonged to one of the pseudo-intellectuals lost in the sea of people on the other side of the door. On this side of the door, though, was where the real fun was about to go down.

Now I know why I'm having this dream—it was also the beginning of the end.

We could hear the chatter beyond the door, the usual chitchat from drunken college kids as they saun-tered by the door, the occasional knock and turn of the knob to see if the room was occupied. Even the noise from the balcony drifted through the curtained and closed window. None of us minded; it was audi-tory camouflage for our carnal activity. The only light coming into the room was a mix of moonlight and streetlamps diffused by the curtain. It made Faith look beautiful; Wanda too. But at this point in the dream, I'm not looking at either Faith or Wanda. Nope. I'm looking at Henry's rock-hard junk. It was a meager five or six inches, with a head that mushroomed out far enough to where it looked like it might get stuck, like a barbed arrow, once he slid inside a girl. That's where my dream picked up at this moment. That's the moment my mind decided it needed to etch into its eternal memory of things relevant and essential— me staring at some dude's oddly shaped, one-eyed purple people-eater.

There I was standing next to Henry. Both of us were facing the ladies with our fists on our hips, elbows out to the sides, and chests puffed up. We looked like some display of reject porn stripper applicants, waiting to be told they weren't good enough for the main stage. Meanwhile, the ladies were comparing notes on the similarities and differences between our (insert not-yet-used-euphemism) ramrods. But we stood there like champions, also comparing notes on our ladies, breast size and shape, vaginal differences, and so on and so forth. But the party was fun so far. There we were, drunk, consenting adults doing what they do in the exploratory phases of life. We proceeded to rail our girls right next to each other on some stranger's bed. A glorious sight it was, watching two pairs of breasts bounce all about as we slid in and out of our respective partners. Four breasts, twice the usual amount one gets to look at while having sex; it was wondrous!

But for the life of me, my brain can't figure out why this moment was the beginning of the end. How could this be the moment it all started going wrong? I'm sure on some level it already was going awry, but this was the catalyst to bring to light that things were not as glorious as Faith and I perhaps thought they were. This moment is what was needed to ultimately push us away and toward the life that we needed and wanted to live.

The next thing I knew, we were all sitting on the bed post-coitus in uncomfortable silence. Henry and I were wiping our manhoods clean while the girls toweled off our self-made love lotion from their chests. It was at this point in my dream that I remember why this was the defining moment. The beginning of the end, if it hadn't already begun—Henry wanted to swap. I was conflicted, not because I didn't understand the concept but because I wanted to do it also, kind of. My alcohol and THC-riddled mind wanted to stick my dick in the girl next to my girl. I craved to double-dip into the girl with slightly larger breasts and a few more freckles everywhere, which would have been okay if Faith wanted to sleep with Henry.

Nope. She didn't even say it out loud. The disgust on her face at the thought of him was enough to tell everyone she was not down for any swapping of any kind.

I wanted Wanda, but Faith just wanted to enjoy the moment we had and not take it any further. So there I sat, too drunk to think about what she wanted and too stoned to realize what was really going on. So, we two guys were trying to pull a partner swap that neither partner truly wanted. Hell, I didn't want Henry to bang Faith, and Wanda's expression was clear she sure as hell didn't want me tossing one in her. We were caught in an awkward situation in which Henry had an idea that I didn't actually want to go through with but would not back down from because of some stupid, miscon-strued sense of machismo, or lack of being adven-turous, or coming off as a lame-o, or some silly crap.

But to the point of the moment, Faith made a joke at my expense. For the love of my memory, I can't remember what she cracked, but I made an off-color joke back at her. (It wasn't so much a joke as it was a sarcastic comment that was meant to be funny but came off as one of the most asshole-y, rude, inappro-priate things I've ever said in my life.) But Faith made the joke, and she laughed. Henry and Wanda laughed, but I didn't laugh. I knew she said it in jest and was meant to be cute, but I was inebriated. I was an ass-hole, an asshat, immature, and not nearly as clever as I thought. As I was putting on my shorts so I could go take a leak, I turned to her and, dripping with the thickest sarcasm I could froth in my mouth, screamed, "Fuck you!"

Here's the thing about it though, I don't know what I was thinking. Maybe I thought I was some sort of sublime comic genius fresh off from watching *Man On The Moon*. Perhaps I should have just stuck with music and left clever to the comics. In that instant, the smiles wiped off their faces. The noise outside the room con-tinued on but, inside that room, the silence was deaf-ening. There was a sick feeling in my stomach. It was quickly overtaking my senses, drowning out my ability to comprehend the reprehensible nature of my words and numbing my ability to feel anything but the growing pain in my gut. Before I could even try to defend my indefensible actions, the swelling pain shot forth from my mouth, landing all over my shorts, the top of the dresser, and inside a few partially opened drawers.

Maybe it was the liquid form of Mike Tyson upper-cutting my insides till it was outside that caused my off-color remark. Perhaps I wasn't the nice guy I deluded myself into thinking I was. Maybe I did mean some-thing by it, but just can't, or don't want to, remember what it was. It doesn't matter; excuses are for the weak. Anyone who tries to preface lousy behavior with some bullshit reason isn't much of a person. Any way it went, I was standing there covered in my own puke.

The thing about Faith is that she didn't hold my words against me. To her, this moment might be just another flaw she overlooked in some misguided ado-ration for me. She hopped up, still in her birthday suit, and made her way to me. In the 3.5 seconds it took for her to reach me, another spout of bile and alcohol spewed forth from my mouth, further covering my bare torso. She was such a kind soul and didn't care that she was still naked. She didn't care about the numerous strangers on the other side of the door. She opened the door, with her arm around me, and headed into the sea of onlookers gawking at the sight of her breasts and my chest hair matted in vomit. She led me to the bathroom, the good girlfriend that she was.

I remember clearly that I sat dry heaving into the toilet while she held my hair out of the line of fire. She sat there, rubbing my back, trying to calm my nerves with quiet whispers. Now, the full-chest heaving (whose low-toned sounds could summon ancient, primordial demons) had possessed my diaphragm in full force. All I wanted to do was calm down so I could try to give Faith some false, off-the-cuff explanation as to why I failed so spectacularly back in the room. But I couldn't. All I could do was sit there and listen to her tell me we'll talk about it later or that everything was going to be okay. All sorts of pleasantries were said to ease the tension of the moment, only to prolong the detonation of whatever explosive the bomb held.

The sounds of Faith's voice continues to echo through my ears, the quiet tones of her calming me down from the nightmare of the moment. I hear her whisper to me that "Everything is fine. It's only a dream." Over and over, the sound of her voice invades my mind more and more, making it seem more real. The dream in my mind that is caught on loop, as I dry heave into a stranger's dirty toilet, becomes more vivid as she keeps whispering over and over the same words that solidify into my mind, "It's only a dream."

The reality of my dream fades away as the waking world starts to come into focus. The blurred lines of dreaming and being awake stay discombobulated, though Faith's words stay brick solid. My eyes flutter open to clear away the cobwebs. I hear new words from Faith. "You're finally awake."

The world comes into focus as the blinding light of day dims. All I can see is Faith, her Mona Lisa smile painted onto her face in a never-ending attempt to pretend that everything is going to be okay.

I don't remember the ambulance. I remember the rain and the crash.

"Did anyone pick up Viv and Logan? Her car broke down. They probably think I'm such an ass." I watch as Faith's face twists at my words.

"Viv and Logan are fine. You don't remember, do you?" Faith starts. The only sounds I hear in between her words are the steady electronic beeps of hospital monitors.

"I remember a bit. What happened?" I am wholly stumped by Faith's words.

The air around us is thick and heavy. The tones of the room have disappeared, leaving only the silence to be broken. She points a hesitant finger at me. "You happened. You've been out a while longer than I think you think."

"What? Did I miss the rest of the party?" I try to add some levity.

Her grimace lets me know that not only is the bachelor party over, but also that jokes are anything other than welcome.

I try to sit up in my bed as a pulling sensation tests the stretching limits of the stitches holding the hole closed that my rib stuck through not too long ago. I lay back down and reach for the bedside remote, slowly raising the back of the bed like some invalid mastermind ruling the world from my internal prison. Well, at least that's what it feels like right now.

I am up.

A little more aware than a few moments ago. An awareness springs to the front of my mind that the bruises are healing and still painful (both to touch and just for being). The blunt, throbbing sensation of a healing bone that feels like it is going to snap back in half at the slightest tap is a new reminder of what I can't clearly remember. And now that I am upright, I will wait for Faith to speak.

"You've been in a drug-induced coma. The rib wasn't the worst of it. The police say there was a multi-car collision, then a secondary hit. That hit took Ronnie, they say. Then a third hit," she says while fighting off tears that well up in her eyes.

I shake my head in disbelief. "Took Ronnie? Where's he at? How's he doing? I don't remember the second hit. I remember the one that knocked Ronnie out."

Her tears break. Faith starts sobbing quietly as tears stream down her cheeks. "He's gone. That second hit messed you up, too."

I try to lean into Faith to give her a hug, but the pain is telling me otherwise. My eyes search the room for anything to help ease the hurt. I find a morphine drip in my left arm and hit the button a few times to help mitigate the sensation, something to make me more comfortable. I extend the better of my two arms and place my hand on her shoulder. She bends her neck to snuggle my hand as she wipes away her tears.

"What do you mean he's gone? And don't tell me he died." I deny what I know is true.

She sniffs up a round of tears, then blurts out in a moment of hysterics. "I thought I was going to lose you. The doctors didn't know how long you'd be unconscious. I was so worried."

"How long? How long was I out for?" I start to remember that I have a tour to manage for Spear Fist. I have a wedding to attend and a career that has people relying on me.

"Five days," she starts as she tries to calm back down, "but the doctors said if you wake, woke, whatever, you should be fine." Faith holds her stomach like an invisible fist punched her square in the gut.

"You all right?" I ask, forgetting the news that catalyzed the crash.

"Doctors say I need to keep calm." The meekness in her voice hopes I remember what she told me. "All the stress is threatening my pregnancy."

"Five days isn't so bad." I realize I missed a few significant milestones in such a short time. "But the tour is starting in less than forty-eight hours, and there's all the final touches, the wedding."

"You missed the wedding. Five days you were out. The wedding was two days after the bachelor party." Faith shakes her head at my narrow-tracked mind. "You're not doing the tour with them. You need to heal; otherwise, you won't be around to do any more tours with anybody."

I move forward as if I had the strength to jump out of bed, but the pain overtakes my body, sending me right back against the mattress. The morphine has either already worn off, or I am in far more pain than these drugs can handle. I hit the feel-good button a few more times.

"Get some rest, love." She bends down to kiss my forehead. "I'll fill you in on everything when you are more awake."

CHAPTER 2

Dance

My first waking night in the hospital is a lonely one. The ambient buzzing and beeping of machines from my room, the noises from the staff as they walk by doing their nightly duties, all seem to be so distant and uncaring. I drift in and out of sleep, constantly waking from pain. The push of my morphine button helps me fall back asleep for a few minutes at a time. I guess five days does not heal broken bones and hard bruises. The endurance of the morphine button to be hit as many times as I have this night is an impressive feat. However, I am pretty sure most of my pressing is an exercise in futility, as I've met my hourly limit of fun drugs at this point.

The few moments I am awake are spent staring at the off-white, acoustic ceiling tiles, as headlights outside cast their shadows in a silent, abstract show eerie enough to scare a small child. The moments between, when my eyes were shut, I drift into a twilight haze where my brain tries to figure out if I am sleeping or awake. I start to dream a few times, but those are quickly cut off as my sleeping mind wants me to adjust, then the pain jolts me awake for a few moments to once again stare at the shadows.

The shadow plays are only a distraction from the thoughts that plague my mind while I lay awake, hoping for sleep. The idea that Ronnie is gone hits me harder than his fist when it first connected with my face weeks ago. While his fist connected quite nicely, I did deserve it. In the end, he was actually a pretty good guy. In the end. I may just be the one to blame for his demise. Had Faith not said over speakerphone what she said while Ronnie was riding shotgun, I wouldn't have dropped the phone and swerved. But I recovered from that; I remember that. His end can't merely be nothing more than the sad conclusion to a series of unfortunate and malicious events. I'm not one to ponder on things. . . oh, who the hell am I kidding? Of course, I am. If I weren't, I would have been able to move on from Faith eighteen years ago when we first split up. I wouldn't be holding onto this notion of who I think she is, or could be, and who I could be that caused all the events to unfold the way they did, causing Ronnie to be riding with me to pick up Viv and her new girl.

Fate is a funny thing.

By the time daylight arrives, I've given up on any sort of sleep. The exhaustion only makes my pain tolerance plummet, exponentially increasing the need for my little morphine button. The thoughts of doing any type of physical rehab or even walking to take a leak are unwelcome.

Lunchtime rolls around faster than I thought. I could have sworn I just woke up and was looking around, but here sits a tray next to my table. My sore muscles and bones lift the lid off my plate to reveal the light brown, wafer-thin patty of mystery meat on an unseasoned, flavorless bun they pass off for a hamburger. Not even a slice of cheese. The side dish of orange juice fortified with iron to give it the taste of a metal spoon is also less than satisfying. But there it is. I must have gone to the bathroom between dawn and now because I don't have to go. I must be more exhausted than I thought.

I close my eyes to take a bite of my sandwich I hesitantly call a burger. A few chews later, and with a swallow, I open my eyes. I repeat this a few times. On my last swallow, however, I open my eyes to a tray-less room. No remnants of my burger or orange juice are left. It's not even daylight anymore; the twilight hour is upon me. The hospital room is lit by the orange-and-purple light of the evening sky. Again, I find myself pressing the morphine button. I'm not sure if my loss of time is due to my pain, some undetected brain injury, sleepiness, the drugs, or a mixture of some or all the above.

For the moment, I am okay with it. I don't have to think about the dead guy I was driving with. I don't have to think about the tour I am missing or any possible impact this may have on my future with Spear Fist or any other band. I don't have to dwell on the pain that Faith must be feeling over her loss. I don't have to think and don't want to remember.

Introspection is bad.

I rest my eyes for a moment just to relax the pain away, but when I open them, the morning is upon me. Next to my bed is last night's mostly untouched dinner I don't remember nibbling on and the food attendant giving me a fresh meal that I'll avoid as long as possible. As he exits the room, a sight for my sore eyes enters with an exhausted smile and a bag with some clothes.

"I have been talking to your doctors. They're a little worried about your pain level. Still, there's physically nothing wrong with you, besides the expected." Faith smiles a little more, extending the bag my direction. "You were out of it last night. I helped myself to a bite of your supper."

A doctor strolls into the room. At least I'm assuming he's a doctor, and my doctor at that, since he has a white coat on, stethoscope around his neck, and a tablet he's tapping away on.

"Good morning, Mr. Fairlane," he says without looking up from his tablet. "I'm writing you a couple of prescriptions for the pain. And your lovely fiancée says she'll fill them so you don't have to."

I give a raised brow to Faith. She shrugs her shoulders, giving me a playful smile. "I'll take good care of him, doctor."

The doctor turns to Faith. "The meds are as needed, but they can be addictive, so use with discretion. If he gets worse, if his energy doesn't pick back up, any of the things we talked about that you said you would rather do from the comfort of your home, you page me and get him back in here."

I huff in amusement that the doctor is giving my fake fiancée a list of things without even acknowledging me.

"Thanks, doc," I interrupt. "I'll be fine. Rest, walk, sleep, repeat until healed," I say, forcing myself to stand up. The pulling pain of the healing stitches catches my attention and shoots any sleep left in me clear out of my head.

The doctor turns back to Faith with a smile. "Have fun. And as I said, page me if you need anything or have any questions." He turns back to me. "She's a good lady to take care of you like this. She could've just let you stay here to recover as recommended. Take care of yourself. I'll see you in six weeks for a check-up."

He exits and, after the nurse removes my morphine IV, Faith helps slide a clean shirt over my head. "Been a long time since you had to take care of me like this."

She shakes her head at my nostalgia. "I remember. Almost eighteen years you managed to not need me to help you." She grabs my pants and starts sliding them up my legs. "That was an interesting night. Let's just get you outta here."

As the drug-addled haze wears thin again, I find myself at home, lying in my bed. I hear Faith in my kitchen and assume she is attempting some sort of dinner.

"Faith!" I call out, trying not to put any strain on my diaphragm.

I hear what I assume to be a metal pot dropping onto the tile floor, "Shit! Coming!" She picks it up, clanking it on the counter.

"How far are you into cooking?" I inquire.

"Not far enough that you can't ask if I'd like to go out for a bite instead." She smirks, gesturing to the door.

The spot we find ourselves in is a Flo-grown burger joint called Adler's, a little place that started off as a food truck and has grown into a brick-and-mortar location. While the burgers aren't as thick as Chicago's own Kuma's Corner, the tastes definitely rival each other. Anyone who's been to a big city like Chicago, New York, San Francisco, or New Orleans knows that big cities have good food, some iconic dish or two that makes it renowned. Florida, especially Orlando, is the opposite of the rule. Food in Florida sucks on a level that you can only understand if you aren't from Florida but have stayed here for an extended period, or inversely, if you grew up here and did extended travel outside of Florida. Orlando is all chain restaurants of mediocre-at-best foods. However, Adler's dares to break such conventions and stands miles above the rest when it comes to Florida food. But that rant aside, we sit in silence as the food is dropped off at our table.

Faith waits for me to bite into my burger before filling me in on the events since the accident. I know she is waiting because her bottom lip keeps ever so slightly twitching, like she is about to speak. I don't know if she is waiting because it's bad news and wants to make me think, chew, and swallow before I respond, or because receiving bad news on an empty stomach makes it that much worse. Whatever her reasoning, I'm okay with her consideration.

"The paramedics or coroner or whoever said that Ronnie was killed in the crash," she slowly starts. "There was nothing anyone could have done."

I try to listen, but she wasn't there. She didn't see the light fade from Ronnie's eyes. Hell, maybe I only think I saw the light fade from his eyes. Conceivably, he was already gone when I saw him. Maybe what I thought was fading light was just him slipping into unconsciousness. The thought of it all sends pains through my broken rib.

Either way, she wasn't there. She continues telling me something more about the accident. My mind shifts attention to the song playing on some local radio station, forcing itself not to remember any more than it already does. I listen to the lyrics as Faith tells me all about the others involved; that it wasn't just Ronnie, but that the police think the driver who killed him was also killed. However, in my mind, none of that matters. Had I only not answered the call, had she not told me she was pregnant, had Viv's truck not broken down, had any of those things not happened, then Ronnie might still be alive. His life wouldn't have been stripped from him. Yes, there's an enormous part of me that thinks it's my fault. I guess only I can take another guy's death and turn it into a moment about me feeling regretful. I am an asshat. Then I hear Faith's words.

"It's not your fault, ya know. It was a bad night," she says, eating another bite of her burger. "It's not like you were trying to get anyone hurt or anything. It just sucks. I lost my Ronnie."

"I'm sorry." What the hell else am I going to say? It's not like I can bring him back. I can't snap my fingers and turn back time. Even Cher can't do that.

"I know you're sorry. But it's not that. When I first arrived at the hospital. . . I didn't know Ronnie had died. I didn't know. I ran to you first." A thick coating of self-hatred covers her words.

There it is: the moment that I have been waiting for since I ran into Faith again. Since our lives have reunited, I have been waiting for some admission or acknowledgment that I am who she really wants to be with. But for the love of all that is sacred, not under these circumstances. Now a seed is planted in the back of my mind, a seed that whispers to me that I did kill him to be with Faith. In all logical thinking, it can't be true simply because of the chronology of the events. But it's planted there and whispers to me, my sweet demise.

A second voice whispers in my other ear that she is only with me now because Ronnie is out of the picture. That had he survived, they would still be together, that I am some sort of morbid consolation prize. A bigger part of me knows these thoughts are some forms of residual Catholic guilt from my childhood, but still, they whisper.

She continues. "Once I found out he was dead, I hated you. I hated you until I realized that I hated myself for running to my ex before running to my fiancé. I didn't know how to process it, so I hated you. I hated myself. But it's not your fault. There's no one to blame here. I wanted to be mad at you. I wanted to loathe you and despise you. I can't, though. I have to forgive myself if I can. But how can I?"

She stops talking, leaving me to wonder if I am supposed to answer that, or if she is speaking rhetorically. If I don't answer and she wants me to, then I'm an ass. If I answer and she doesn't want me to, then I am self-absorbed or self-satisfying, or whatever the appropriate phrase is that I can't think of right now. But even if I choose not to decide, I still made a choice, right?

"Time. Everything in time," I offer up a humble response. But the Sweet Blood song "Dance" on the radio reminds me that it is most likely too late to be forgiven, or will even that change with time for her? I take a pain pill (or two or three) out of my pocket and toss them down my throat.

She laughs, shaking her head. "Only you can sum up something so complex and gut-wrenching with such a simple answer and expect others to suddenly be okay. Life's not that simple."

I chew a bite of burger. "Never said it was simple. Just because I say something that sounds simple doesn't mean I expect it to be taken so simply. Everything takes time, including the digestion of those simple words."

Her eyes squint as if looking deep into her own mind for a moment before biting into her burger. We sit in comfortable silence for a few, long minutes.

"The day after it all happened, I had a long talk with Jacquelyn." Faith hesitates as she treads forth.

"Comparing notes?" I jest.

"You could say that. From how Jacquelyn made it sound, you really seem to like her," Faith puts out there, hoping for a negation of her suspicions.

"She treats me well. Not as well as others, but I haven't seen her since the bachelor party," I say.

A smile crosses Faith's face as she takes the last bite of her burger. "Heard about that, too. Must have been an interesting sight to find your girl straddling D.B.'s face for a five-spot."

"It was a twenty note, thank you very much." I laugh. The ludicrousness of it all sets in.

"It could have been a fifty, but the way she felt when she saw your face made it all worthless, she said," Faith continues.

I swallow the last bite of my burger. "That's good to know. So, why hasn't Jacquelyn come to visit?"

"That's what we talked about, after the funeral," Faith ventures onward.

"What? You had his funeral without me?" I snap.

She puts a hand up. "Woah. No one knew when, or if, you were going to come to, wake up, whatever. So yeah, bodies can only be preserved well for so long."

"Point taken," I concede to another missed milestone.

"As I was saying, after the funeral, we got things in order for the tour." She pauses, knowing damn well I'm about to say something.

"Who, how, when?" I throw out a few words to chew on.

"Well, Mr. Fancypants. I went into your place and got your datebooks, notes, notepads, etc., etc. Viv and I figured it all out. Made a few calls and changed some things."

"I needed that money from the tour," I say in a moment of ungraciousness.

"You'll get most of it still. A thank-you-for-doing-my-job-for-me-when-I-was-in-a- fuckin'-coma-or-whatever-even-though-you-don't-know-what-you're-doing would be nice," Faith reminds me.

"Of course. I don't know why I said that. I'm sorry. Thank you very much for all that," I apologize. "Viv helped?"

"Viv's actually on tour with them, acting as the manager while you rest here. She and Logan wanted to be together anyway. Logan says Viv is her muse," Faith continues.

"And D.B. and the guys? They're okay with this?" I ask.

"Of course they'd rather have you. Hell, Viv would rather it be you, but she's there because you're here. Now all you have is me." Faith smiles. Her eyes search for a glint of gratitude in mine but only sees the searching within. My eyes scour my thoughts on what I need to do next, for whatever the thing is that will help me forget my life is figuratively over while the guy who was kind enough to ride with me—his life is over.

Again, I know in my heart of hearts it's not my fault, but damn if it doesn't feel like it should have been me. Ronnie should have had the happily ever after with Faith. With me out of the picture, there'd be no nagging devil on her shoulder, poking at her to do the Finn Fairlane thing instead of the right thing. But he's gone, and she's left with me. I hardly call this the beginning of a happily ever after, but it is what it is. God, I hate that statement. It is what it is. It couldn't be vaguer and more general if it tried.

I sit, trying to take in everything she told me, the fact that my life came to a sudden, and possibly permanent, standstill. How someone who has no experience with tour management is handling my tour solely based on my ledgers and notes. Ronnie is dead, and somehow, I end up rewarded for it. Not cool. Can't be good karma. Then a thought hits me. Faith never finished telling me what happened between her and Jacquelyn. "So, is she mad at me?" I ask.

Faith shakes her head. "No. No one can ever stay mad at you. That's the great enigma of being Finn Fairlane. No matter what childish, stupid, or immature thing it is that you do, somehow, it's never actually your fault. You have the gift of always being in the wrong place at the right time. The smile on your face is so disarming that it just washes away the anger people may feel at the moment toward you. Jacquelyn, though, I think in the end, she wants what's best for you. Or at least she wants you to want what you want. If that makes any sense."

I hear her words, and in some convoluted way, her words make perfectly clear sense. But she said, "in the end."

"What do you mean, 'in the end'?" I press.

"It means we talked. We came to an understanding," Faith says.

When someone says those words, it can mean only two things: one, they actually did come to an understanding, or two, Faith forced Jacquelyn to come to the conclusion she wanted Jacquelyn to arrive at—Faith's conclusion. With Faith, both options are entirely plausible.

"By the time we were finished, I think she understood my needs. Not my needs as a woman or any crap like that. My needs as a human. I can't be without Ronnie and without you. I need someone there for me, someone who understands," she confesses.

Now I know I shouldn't feel like she is using me as some sort of healing salve to rub on her as she feels the need, but I kind of do. Perhaps, this is the karmic payback I must settle in my own way. Or maybe she should talk to and spend a week with her sister.

"Where's Jeanine in all of this?" I coldly ask.

"Fuck, Finn," she says, the tone of my words stabs at her. "After the wedding, she and Gregg decided she should go with."

I shake my head a little. "So, that quickly now she already has him on a tight leash."

I should be careful when I cook up my words because I know I am often forced to chew and swallow them.

"God, you're such an asshole sometimes. She, Gregg, and the almighty D.B. actually thought it'd be nice to have someone along who can help with everything. She's there to make sure Viv is good. That the bands are good. She put her life on hold for you," she scorns, deservedly so. I am an ass.

"How was the wedding?" I steer the subject a bit to the left.

"Short a groomsman. The guy wouldn't get out of bed," she jokes.

"I needed my sleep. No objections or trashtastic fights?"

She lets out the first real laugh since I woke up. "No. Nothing like. . . God, whose wedding was that anyway?"

I laugh through the pain in my ribs. "Wally and Lynn. Back in, like, 2000," I remind her.

"That's right!" she says, waving her hands. "Some guy saw his girlfriend dancing with. . . what's his name?"

"Yup. He found out they had slept together a few weeks earlier. He was pissed," I continue the story.

"And a fight almost broke out, but everyone stood up for the homewrecker, not the guy who got cheated on," Faith finished up.

"What a night!" My exclamation aggravates my chest pain.

"Who would have known that evening would have been a foreshadowing of things to come for us!" she tries to say with enthusiasm, but the sad reality of her words sinks in for both of us.

So here we sit, in Adler's, our bellies full of great burgers as we wonder what the future holds. And yes, it is a scary thought for both of us.

I feel the pain flaring up. The intensity quickly rises, so I grab a few more Vicodin and fling them down my throat. Anything to make it all go away.

CHAPTER 3

Times Like These

The harsh light of day rears its ugly head. The early morning light that sneaks in between the curtains stabs me directly in the eyes. I look over and squint so the lovely woman lying next to me can come into focus. For a moment, the pain is gone: no broken ribs, no deep bruises, no healing cuts or scrapes. I can't even feel the persistent, throbbing headache I've inherited since I woke from the accident. All of it disappears when I see her. My love, my Faith. She's come home. Perhaps she's always been there, and it's I who have finally returned. No matter; we are together.

As much as the pain disappears when I see her, I know it is still there. Faith is but a safe place, an oasis in the desert, a pill to further numb the pain. But like all things, the pain returns when the release ends. I reach for my diminishing supply of pain pills, ever standing at attention, awaiting my return on the nightstand, much like my late dog, Lt. Dan, used to wait for me. How I miss that mangy dog. The pain floods back in, filling every cell of my body. I could say it seems a little less this time around, though that's like saying 215-degree water is colder than 300. It's boiling and can still kill you or, at the very least, scar you for life. But that's where I am right now.

I peek over to the old alarm clock radio next to my bed. It's the clunky radio from back in the day, the one with the oversized red digital display, yet has the durability to be thrown across the room when you just didn't want to hit snooze for the twentieth-somethingth time. It reads 7:30 a.m., way too early for the likes of a night owl such as myself to rise and shine. Faith, however, shall be answering the call of the alarm in a few. Her work in the salon is never done, which means I'll have to fend for myself until she gets home. That means having to get from point A to point B, if needed. I order an Uber as I crawl out of bed. Rise and shine I must and deal with this day. I think the best way to do that is to swallow the pain pills I've been holding onto. A hazy Uber ride later, I find myself at a car dealership, as it is a day to fend for myself and a day spent buying a car. A short search leads me to a Pontiac not too far removed from mine that was recently totaled.

A slightly less hazy ride home and I head back to bed. Faith is already at work, and I can't even fathom how long I've been up. The next thing I know, I hear the sweet sound of Faith telling me it's 6:00 p.m., and I need to wake the fuck up. Ever the gentle soul she can be.

"Come on, Daddy. Taking care of your ass while growing this thing inside me ain't the easiest thing, ya know." She hints at my impending fatherhood.

The jolt of that reminder wakes me from my fog but only further seats the realization that I am neither fit for Faith nor fatherhood. I don't want to be Abel to her Cain. It's not fair to her or the unborn. Plus, it didn't end well for Abel. I know the pain is waiting to creep back in at the most unexpected moment, so I want to get ahead of it. Get a jump on keeping it at bay before I get knocked down. I'll get up again, though. No pain is ever gonna keep me down. I know that because of the two pills I just swallowed. Here I go, 6 p.m. and my day is beginning, again.

While the pain has subsided since waking, it's still a thick fog hovering just below sight—noticeable in the peripheral and kicking up with movement. The thoughts of the tour, venues, hotels, and stops along the way all kick up a bit in the fog. I know they are taken care of and know Viv is probably doing a stellar job with my tour, but it's my tour. My career. It's the nights like those that I live for: the stage lights burning my eyes, the sound of the feedback bleeding my ears, the adrenaline racing through my veins with such force that I think my heart might explode. What I am doing right now, sitting at a dinner table eating Chinese take-out while reruns of *How I Met Your Mother* sound off in the background, is not my idea of what I want to be doing tonight. It's not my idea of what I want to be doing any night. Being on the road, you grow accustomed to eating cigarette-smoked bar and hotel food, sleeping in beds you never want to look at under a black light, and driving in a car, van, or bus more than living in a house. It's a lifestyle, and it's the only one I've looked forward to since I began touring. It is my time, and it was taken from me by some jackass who can't understand braking distance in the rain, and the second and third jackass who also can't drive.

That is Orlando, the place where dreams are swallowed by the highway system that leads to the only place here allowed to dream. The destination that makes dreams come true, if only they did come true down here. At least I'm pretty sure Florida isn't filled with people who wished for a fourth-rate educational system, meth addiction, and inadequate employment opportunities. But it is what it wants to be: gilded for anyone staying less than two months, a snowbird escape for six, and a twisted reality for anyone who lives year-round, and definitely not how I envision any future I may have with Faith.

"Whatcha thinking about?" Faith slurps up some lo mein.

"Whaddya mean?" I twirl my noodles.

She chuckles a bit. "Your mile-long stare is a neon sign of unspoken thoughts."

"Thinking about the tour. I need this rib to heal, and whatever internal swelling might still be swollen to go down so I can catch up with Spear Fist. I need to figure out what's going on with you and me, I, us. You know. We got this thing growing inside you, and I haven't had any time to process the news. I haven't reacted to it myself yet. I don't know how you want me to react. It's just so much in so little time," I say in a moment of blunt honesty.

Faith drops her fork, the clanging sound of which sends jolts of pain through my left temple. She tilts her head and squints her eyes. The razors shooting out of them cut right through me. "How I want you to react? I want you to react however you react. I don't want some lame, forced reaction of joy if the thought of fatherhood makes you want to run for the hills."

My neon sign of thoughts is shattered into a million pieces by Faith's words and the growing pain that runs through me. It's not like the thought of being a dad makes me want to run a one-way marathon out of town that only Forrest Gump could be proud of. It's just an idea that I never put much thought into. I make music; that is it. I know it's not like musicians are all childless heathens who shun the idea of reproducing. Some of them have wives and children they see regularly and are part of their lives. Some are good parents. I just never was one to think that the title of father would be mine one day.

"I don't want to run for the hills." I laugh. "I'm actually excited, I think. Nervous maybe. I don't know exactly, but I'm definitely in it."

"In it? As in not running, not leaving me behind, not forgetting we exist?" she says with an unreadable facial expression. "I guess that's a start."

"Did you think I was that guy to do something like that?" I tease.

"What guy?" she plays coy.

"Don't give me that 'what guy?' bull," I say with a pointed fork. "You thought I was that guy. The guy that disappears when he finds out his penis works properly. The guy that sticks it in anything wet, without any thought or regard to the consequences that may follow for the fairer sex. You thought I was him."

She laughs through a bite of food. "Maybe a little, sure. But can you blame me? Look at your past. Our past."

"Why? Did you read somewhere that I have a love child running around somewhere I've never been told about? Or love children?" I inquire.

"No," she chuckles. Her laughter helps my pain subside a little. "I mean, over a decade of rock 'n roll decadence doesn't exactly extol the virtues of a housewife, husband, whatever."

"That's a blanket statement if ever there was one." I laugh through my bite of food.

"Hey, at least I know you want to be on board," she defends.

"Plus, there are good family men among the rock crowd. Bon Jovi for one," I say, semi-jokingly.

"Come on, Finn. You can't expect to stay the man you were," she throws out a curveball.

"And you can't expect me to change. You know who I am and who I was going into this," I defend.

"You know, Finn. You don't make things easy. I'm doing this for more than some, still hypothetical, baby. I'm doing this for you, and yes, for me, too. Maybe I need you. Ever think of that?" Faith fires off.

It has crossed my mind. I just don't think I've given it as much thought as I should have if I'm back to thinking about the entirety of the entity known as Faith and Finn again. *Damn, so what's a boy to do? I have obligations. I have a life. I have the woman I've wanted more than anything else. I have a to-be child in that woman. How can I make this work? Oh, what's this boy to do?*

Here's what I do know: I love this woman. I've said it before, and I'll say it again. I love this woman and always have. No matter how bad the times got back in the day or how good they were, my love for her never waned. It never faltered—my love, that is. I am sure I fucked up in many ways many, many times, but that's one of the many reasons I love her so. No matter how many times I faltered, she was always there. Well, until the end, of course, but a man can only be given so many opportunities. Apparently, though, after eighteen years, my chances have replenished like the seven-year abstinence thing that makes you a virgin again…so I hear.

"I didn't. There's something in me that hoped you still needed me or had feelings or whatever you wanna call it. But after the years had gone by, I figured I was just another mistake." I finish off my meal.

"My favorite, if one can have a favorite mistake." She smiles back. "So, what do we do?"

She stares at me, a little lost in her thoughts and, possibly, a little scared while waiting for an answer. I know she doesn't want a repeat of our past. I guess neither do I. It's just that I find myself in unfortunate situations. Fun, sure, but unfortunate, and I think that's what she's afraid of, more of the same from the man known as Finn. My rib is starting to throb while watching her wheels turn. I don't like it. I reach for my pills and swallow one, hoping it helps this time. I'm still waiting for an answer from her, though I don't think I'll be getting one anytime soon.

So, it boils down to her question. . . "What do we do?" I don't think something that universally profound can be answered while eating take-out lo mein. I'm not even sure if it can ever be answered, but I must try if I don't want her to leave me again, if I want this thing between us to work. If I am ever to get this crazy little thing we call love and life right, it has to be now. This is my second chance. While most people never get one, no one ever gets a third. So, this is it. I'm not sure exactly what needs to be done or how to get there, but if this is ever going to work, now is the time to get it right. Here's the thing of it all—we have to figure out the "what do we do" of it all. I have to decide if I can leave the life I love behind for her, but I have no idea about anything.

CHAPTER 4

Going Out Strange

There was something about my old lady and me sloppin' down food, trying to figure out second chances, that made me think of a guy I met once upon a time. My meeting with him had nothing to do with Chinese food, but with the need for a second chance with no clear way to make it work. We were both in the psych ward for different issues. He had been there for close to two months while I had just gotten admitted. I guess if I am going to tell you this story, I need to tell you how I ended up spending seventy-two wonderful hours in the Lutheran General Psych Ward.

It was at the end of the final leg of my band's Tweaker tour, right after Marty and his family died. It was supposed to be the happiest of times; it was not. No matter how many girls flashed their breasts at me while I was on stage, no matter how many fans showered me with some sort of adoration, no matter how good everything was at the time, all I could think about was my friend and his family. Marty was a guy who flowed in and out of my life, but no matter how long it had been since we had seen each other, we picked up like no time had passed. He knew my songs before anyone else, even helping with lyrics on a few random occasions. He could spin a story on the spot just for the entertainment value but tell it with such unparalleled conviction that everyone in the room would eat it up like it was fact. At the end of the story, he, and everyone else, would have a good laugh over the thing.

Even though they were just suckered into believing whatever tale he spun, they'd still laugh. He had that sort of disarming smile, dimples and all.

But back to the point, the tour was over. The rest of the band and road crew were celebrating on the record company's dime. I was sitting on the floor, leaning against the wall in some Chicago suburb bar. I wasn't looking at anyone; I wasn't enjoying the moment. There were no trees that made a forest for me to see. No flowers to stop and smell. Just a dirty bar floor in need of a good mopping and a bar that could use a power wash.

The thing about it is that when everything seems fine, or at the very least, should seem okay, it rarely ever is. All the fans that pass by spraying misguided love on you feels empty. Sure, it's quaint, the gesture anyhow. But it's empty. They don't know you. They don't know what's going on in your world, not outside of what they read in magazine articles or listen to on the radio or in podcasts. So, they give you a compliment and continue on their merry way, thinking the words they say somehow lift you up on a cloud and carry you through until the next praise. But in fact, all it does is shine a light in your eye that feebly attempts to blind you from reality while the metaphorical shit is still hitting the fan. That's what was happening in my life at that moment; the shit just kept hitting the emotional fan.

I was sitting there, sipping on some drink, or three, or five, and I heard a voice. I don't remember who it was, or even if it was male or female, but I heard a voice, "You doin' okay?"

"I wish I was with Marty right now." It's what I said. It's what I meant, but not in the way it was taken.

There was never a moment where I thought I was better off dead or didn't want to be alive anymore. Never did I want to leave it all behind or take a permanent solution, but I did want to be with him. Though, in hindsight, the wording would have been better had I said I wished he was with me at that moment—at that bar with us is what I meant. All I meant was that I wanted him here celebrating with us, but it came out wrong. Maybe I said it the way I said it out of grief. But no matter the reason I said it like that, I did.

The next thing I know, the guys in the band are all hovering over me, drinks in hand. Someone off to the side has their face partially concealed by their cellphone. I hear them talking on the phone about someone making suicidal threats and being clearly depressed. I know they were talking about me, but every sentence the phone person said was carefully constructed to be as non-threatening toward me as possible, as if I was going to stand up and chug down a 1.75 of tequila in one glug to end it all.

I tried telling the mysterious phone person that I was okay, and nothing terrible was going to happen. Still, some sensitive soul had already decided that the world may end if they didn't do everything possible, and over the top, to try and diffuse the situation. All they were doing, in their righteous obliviousness, was making things worse. So, I thought, *Hell, maybe I did say something more than I remember.* It was so damn long ago.

The furious sound of the sirens and blinding reds and whites of the ambulance lights filled the room, muffling the chatter and music of the bar. Two guys in full uniform, ready-to-be-single-serving-friends sat by my side, trying to determine if I was suicidal or not. I wasn't in a great mood, and when you're not in a great mood, the last thing you want is to be bothered by inane questions. I was pissed but not at the EMTs. They were just doing their jobs, paid to be concerned for the welfare of strangers and then take them to a place that can take better care of them than they can themselves. (Did you stay with me on that word mess?) So, questions they asked and answered I did— in a most sarcastic and hostile way. They should have questioned the person that was on the phone. Anyone who is excessively over concerned for another human, unable to tell the difference between suicidal state and mourning depression, needs more serious help than I ever did.

As the fates will have it, it was I that ended up in the ambulance on my way for a minimum of seventy-two-hours of observation. The ride to the ward itself has no place in my memory. I can only assume it was mundane and insignificant in the bigger scheme of things. After I was checked in was when I got a chance to meet Christian. This was a kid—he said he was twenty-three—but the nurses always shook their heads "no." I managed to get one worker to tell me Christian was only twenty. Not sure who was telling the truth or why someone felt the need to lie about it, but stranger things do happen. Age aside, this was a young kid with unkempt, thick, wavy hair in need of proper washing. He was allowed to carry a dry erase marker around with him so he could draw spirals and Fibonacci sequences. Christian had a strange obsession with those two things. I'm not sure if he was schizo or something, but he talked about the irrelevance of time and the meaninglessness of it all.

Maybe that's why this memory has sprung forth in my mind, to remind me of the talks of time and its irrelevant meaninglessness. Or my brain has finally realized that the discussions I had in a seventy-two-hour psych ward window needed to surface. That way, they could point out to me some long-lost lesson that is now relevant in my life, still yet unseen to me.

That's the point, though.

Christian and I sat there in the psych ward's common room while the television droned in the background as Angelina Jolie accepted her win for *Girl, Interrupted*. That's the only part of the award show that stuck in my memory. It could be something about an actress winning an award for a movie about being in a psychiatric institution while sitting in a psych ward, watching her accept that award. Thinking of the chronology of it, it may have been a rebroadcast for some other show, but I stand by my point. There were others in the room, mostly drug addicts slowly detoxing. They were the ones sitting quietly on their best behavior, praying they got out in another day or two. Then, they could score another hit since they were getting no real help there. A few others in there were actual psych patients with severe social disorders, bulimia, anorexia, or whatnot. Others, the real lifers, would just sit in a stereotypical fashion mumbling to themselves while swaying back and forth.

Back to the point, Christian and I sat, talking about time and how, from our perspective, we sit on a rock beneath blue skies. Still, the blue skies are actually infinitely expansive space. The rock we sit on actually travels in a forward motion, spiraling through the universe while spinning in a circle. This means we are literally always in a different spot in the universe every moment of every day. So, what does this all mean concerning Faith? I guess it means we were never in the same place as we were from the first night we met. We were always moving forward, just like this planet of ours, ever-changing and refining ourselves, just like our place in the universe.

What we didn't see, or at least what I didn't see, was how strangely we were going out while we were ending, who we were or had become. Not that anyone ever thinks they've become something so drastically different than who they were, but we do. We all slowly change and metamorphose into these new beings, much like our place in the universe is ever-changing.

We look around the world in which we live, and the surroundings all look the same: the forest still has trees,
the roads are filled with cars, and the drive-thru windows are staffed fully with uninspired teens working
for video game money. In the bigger picture, though,
we are in a completely different spot than we were a
day ago, and more so than a year or ten years ago.
We shoot through this universe at 1.3 million miles
an hour, so we are continually changing at that rate.

It's hard to comprehend, but it's there. Truth from
the mind of a paranoid schizophrenic or whatever he
was. The problem isn't trying to understand the theory.
It sinks in after marinating in your thoughts for far too
long, but it eventually clicks. The sad part of it all is
what you miss in between the introduction and the
end, how life all transpires and how strange it all is.

It started as me finding someone who intrigued me.
Something about Faith hit a funny bone, so I stayed
to explore why it tickled me so. She was intrigued by
me for God knows what reason. Hell, looking back, I'm
not even sure why she stayed or how I fascinated her
enough to stick around, but she did. And for whatever
reason, no matter how we grew, evolved, changed,
whatever, we still stuck around until the bitter end.

The end, much like looking at your immediate
surroundings, is never as simple as it seems. What
was the end eighteen some years ago is now just a
paused moment in our relationship. And here we are
now, some 204,984,000,000 miles away from where
we were in the universe back then. But if you looked
at our surroundings, we appear to be only 1,700 miles
or so away from where we were. Perhaps a little older

and wiser, but not that far, except we can't go back. We can only go forward. I think that's what that crazy guy in the psych ward was trying to tell me. No matter what happens, you can't go home again. There is no going back, only the forward motion. That's not to say things can't work out. Life can be happy and have a happy ending, as long as you don't try to travel back in time. And so the pause button on our relationship has been un-paused in a big way.

Paused relationships proved Christian's theory of time's irrelevance. Much like my friendship with Marty was able to pick up right where we left off, no matter how long it had been, my relationship with Faith seemed to do something similar, as if all the time between our first big breakup simply never happened in that sector of our minds. For when that fateful night occurred, not outside Old Town, but the restaurant bushes, we were all those billions of miles back with just each other. And yes, it was just as awkward as where we left it. But time marches on and so did we. So when we met, even though the feelings were still there and she did not forget what happened, she had moved on, at least enough to forgive and grow. So, all that time between didn't matter. It was meaningless to a point, and irrelevant in the big picture, because here we are.

To think, all of this is because of Chinese food and noodles. Hell, the mind works in mysterious ways. So, you're probably wondering how the hell all this actually relates to Christian. I'll tell ya, it wasn't like me and the cuckoo exchanged numbers while in the ward, but a good conversation can burn someone's face into your mind. After all our talking, I was twice convinced he would never see the outside of a psychiatric institution, except for maybe in transit from one hospital to another.

A good five years or so later, I was out at some bar/saloon in a far outlying Chicago suburb. I can't even remember who the hell I was with at the time. It was either an old bandmate from years earlier or some girl who reminded me of a celebrity. No matter to the story, though. We were surrounded by a few hundred people dressed in their best hair metal band attire, singing along to a Bon Jovi cover band called Bad Medicine. I look over to the bar and see, sitting off on a corner stool with no one around him like he was some pariah, none other than Christian from the ward. He was eating lo mein out of a Chinese to-go container. That must have been why this memory surfaced.

Christian's hard lines and sunken cheeks told me that his time out of the ward had been anything but good to him. I watched as he looked around the bar like some ninja was stalking him. However, no ninja was to be seen. Either he was crazy, or there was a highly skilled ninja skulking about. He had a few empty shot glasses in front of him and a mixed drink of some sort he was nursing in his hand.

The band had just finished playing, "Wanted Dead Or Alive" and started that song from *Young Guns*, "Blaze of Glory." It was about that time I saw Christian get up from his stool. The dim lights of the venue and flashing strobes made him look all the more ominous. He finished off his drink and looked out the windowed doors to a small group of leather-clad men standing next to a few motorcycles.

Now I've seen some strange shit in my life. I saw a guy gorgeously crash his motorcycle and slide a good fifty feet on his face across hot asphalt. No, he did not live. It was a sad sight to see. But a motorcycle crash, while never a way anyone wants to go out, is not a strange way to go. Another time, I was walking through some back street in L.A. and saw a guy get jumped by a group of people. While I didn't see him die, the gunshot I heard gave me a pretty reliable clue that he did. Not sure why they didn't try to take care of me as a witness, but they left me alone. Maybe it was the fact I was stumbling drunk and couldn't identify them for all the money in the world. But this night, at the show, I was debating whether or not I should say something to Christian.

I'm glad I chose nay.

As he approached the door, I saw him squat down and take a quick look around. He didn't see me, or if he did, he recognized me but figured I'd not inter-fere. He then pulled up his pant leg a little bit and pulled something out. I could only figure it was a gun based on where he was fidgeting around. I just figured it was. I knew he was crazy but didn't think he was that crazy. As soon as the door shut behind him, he headed straight to the leather-clad bikers. They didn't even get a chance to see who approached when he started shooting them in their heads. They dropped to the ground like rag dolls. I could feel the jolt of bone against solid blacktop shoot through my head as each victim slammed down. After the last of them fell, the bouncers were running at him, fearless for what would happen to them. It didn't matter though; he turned the gun on himself. A quick fraction of a second and the gun was against his throat, pointed toward the sky. He pulled the trigger, without hesitation, and was gone. Just like that. Gone.

Here was a guy with theories on time and space that were utterly mind-boggling but ended up a blurb in the weekend post. A late-night news story for the masses until the next radar blip. It makes me wonder about his time in between. I pondered where he was in the big picture of things from the time in the ward till that night. While my time between Faith and mine's first departure and our second meeting is irrelevant to the big picture (as far as I can tell), this guy's time between the psych ward and that saloon seem quite relevant to the story. Whatever story that might be, I am sure someone was supposed to take care of Christian. The things that must have happened to make that go awry. The details of his therapy, the trials, the tribulations of this wretched guy's life, everything that ensued led to that point. All those things are anything but meaningless, so many questions to answer to figure out how he ended up where he did. The end of his life was more tragic than our introduction.

Any way you look at it, that was going out as strange as one could go, which finally brings me back to Chinese food and Faith. If I am leaving the music industry, I have to decide how I am going out. If I am to make it work with Faith this time around, I need to figure out how it is going to work. I may need to let go of the past two decades of debauchery and decadence. I will need to devise a way to keep my clients, lest I'll have to hand them off, or at the very least, hand off Spear Fist to someone else. I'll have to decide if someone will take my place in the industry. Pass the torch, so to speak.

However, I am not sure I can leave it behind. I want Faith, sure. She is pretty convinced that I won't make a good father if I stay in the industry. Hell, I could have stopped at father, as in she thinks I won't make a good father, but she has implied she thinks I will magically be a great dad if I leave it behind. Thinking about the convolutedness of it all is maddening. However, the industry is what I love. It's what I know. There's a self-righteous part of me that thinks the world needs me. I can't abandon the world that I helped shape. I would be a selfish person if I left it all behind. One who wants happiness, sure, life on the road seems happy, with late-night, coke-binge, alcohol orgies that blur into each other. But that cannot be true happiness. The equation can't be as simple as fun=happiness. Once upon a time, I would say yes. But I was so much younger then. What I need to figure out is if there is a way to have both. Perhaps that is the pipe dream.

All I know is that right now, at this moment, my body is calling for relief. I reach into my pocket and pull out a bottle of pills. One of the few great joys in life is a good friend and a bottle of pills. I think that thought and immediately know I am deluding myself. But there's a small part of me that thinks maybe I'm onto something. Maybe artists like Amy Winehouse were onto something besides live fast, die young, good-looking corpse bullshit we all daydream about.

But a good-looking corpse does not make a good companion for the living. In the long run, I haven't the slightest clue as to what to do. So, at this moment, I'm going to swallow a couple of these little guys to help ease the pain.

CHAPTER 5

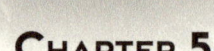

Last Dance With Mary Jane

The incessant nagging of my cellphone tugs at my sleep like an impatient child waking his parents for the day's first meal. I crack open an eyelid to meet the harsh light of day breaking through the drawn shades of my bedroom. I realize I must have been out a little longer than intended from last night's pill-popping.

I pick up my cellphone, but voicemail answers once again. I open my other eye to see a notification for twenty missed calls. Before I can check who they are all from, the phone lights up again, followed by the loud, petulant whining of the ringtone. I swipe up to answer and notice a note that was placed under my phone.

"Hello?" I say to the caller, as I lift up the note.

"I've been calling you non-stop! Why haven't you picked up?!" the voice on the other end shouts.

Rubbing the rest of the sleep from my eyes, I ask, "Viv?"

"Yes, Viv! Finn! We need you! You need to come to New York!" she pleads from hundreds of miles away.

"Yeah, okay. Let me just hop on the first flight I can find," I joke.

"Cool! Let me know the info." She starts to calm down.

"Woah. I was kidding," I say, waving my hands like Viv can see me. "Slow down and start from the beginning."

The hangover from the pills drags me back down. I slump into my pillow.

"So, I had a meeting with some record company guys. They want to work out a deal, like now." Vivian starts from somewhere in the middle of her story. "We're in New York currently. The guys were doing a show when I get a tap on the shoulder."

"Okay. I'm following so far," I say, trying to keep Viv on track.

"It was one of the labels who was at the release show. They want you," Viv says.

And there it is. The words that shall draw me into the scene I know so well, and so far away from where Faith wants me to be. Now to figure out what to do. I have obligations. Viv needs me there to push this deal through—if it's as good as her excitement leads me to believe. Faith needs me, and I need Faith more. I can make this work, though.

"No, 'how are you?' No, 'how are you feeling since being in a drug-induced coma?' Nothing?" I jab at her.

"Faith has been keeping me in the loop in case a situation like this arose, arises, whatever. And it rose. So?" she rapid fires back at me with a sudden stop.

I take a deep breath because she already knows the answer. I turn to sit upright in bed and grab the pill bottle on the nightstand to down a pain pill or three. "I'll text you the flight info."

After booking my flight for later that day and packing my bags, I make the surprisingly uncomfortable drive to Faith's salon. Not that traffic is any worse than usual; it's just that my bones don't seem to be healing as fast or as well as they should. Two decades of decadence might be catching up. I pop four ibuprofens before heading into the salon, hoping the grimace on my face is wiped clean.

The front desk girl is dressed edgy but cute, a compliment to the decor and atmosphere of the salon. It's as if a bar that played rock 'n roll decided to cut hair. I approve.

"Welcome to Medusa's Cut & Color. Do you have an appointment, sir?" The overly excited girl greets me with a smile.

"Is Faith here?" I ask. "I need to speak with her."

"Is this about an appointment? I can help with that." She seems far too eager to be chill.

"No," I say, shaking my head. "It's personal."

A change shifts in her look as she makes a realization. "Oh! You must be Finn! I've heard so much about you! She's in back. You're good to head back there."

The lack of any negative tones in that sentence has me wondering what Faith leaves out of her stories.

"Thank you," I say as I make my way around the reception desk and wall that hides the interior of the salon.

The inside is not what you'd expect for a salon. Instead of bright or even more neutral colors, the owners have opted for deep reds in varying hues and brown trims. A very goth look, but one that is well lit so the stylists can see their work. Seven stylists are working on either cuts or colors, all of whom are in torn jeans and dark-colored shirts. Of course, they have aprons on to protect their clothes. The casual dress style makes this place seem like a place I'd like to get a cut. I wonder why she never told me about this place, perhaps to keep me away from a safe spot for her. Maybe something else. I see three empty chairs and assume one of them is Faith's.

At the far end of the cutting chairs, I stand at the entrance to the back room. I see Faith sitting at a table, her face buried in her phone. I knock on the doorjamb to get her attention. She looks up at me and immediately knows that the news is not what she is wanting to hear.

"It's not as bad as you think," I start.

She laughs to keep herself from getting frustrated. "What?"

Too short to be sweet.

"Viv called me. I have to tie up some loose ends with the band. Add to our future securities," I start with a smile.

"Don't smirk at me, hoping I can guess what you need. Just tell me," Faith says with tightened lips.

"Can you drive me to the airport when you are done for the day?" I respond.

"What?! Why the fuck are you flying anywhere?!" She jumps my shit at that, but I guess I could have eased in with more caution. I mean, who doesn't like a little lube?

"Viv never called you?" I ask.

"Nope." She shakes her head.

"Jeanine?"

"Not about whatever the hell this is." She shakes her head some more.

"Spear Fist is in negotiations. They want me to help iron out the details," I start. "Honestly, shouldn't be more than a week or two max."

I can tell she's pissed. The look on her face tells me so, but she doesn't want to say anything. I sure as hell am not gonna start a fight at her work. Even I'm not that petty. I think we are beyond that stage by now.

"I don't have any more appointments today. Let me see if I can cut out early," Faith offers.

"I don't have to be there for a while," I start.

"It's a slow day here anyway. Shouldn't be an issue," she says with a restrained voice.

I stay toward the back as she walks up to a stylist who's slapping color onto a middle-aged lady's hair. A few words are said back and forth. I try not to stare, so I turn my head to watch them in my peripheral vision. I see her point to me, and her boss laughs. She nods, giving Faith the okay. Faith quickly closes up her station before we head to her car.

"We'll drop my car off at home, then I'll take you to the airport," she says.

On the drive back home, I stay behind her. Not out of caution or to make sure she is safe, but to let her lead and control the pace. I figure if she needs to take some time to think about things, I should give it to her.

"I wanted out early anyway. I was hoping to get some extra time with you today," Faith says in a better state of mind as she steps out of her car back home. "Didn't you get my note?"

I shake my head. "Didn't get a chance to read it. Got distracted by the call. But as I said, I still have a little time. What did you have in mind?" I ask, a little curious about her thoughts.

"Wasn't sure exactly. I just know that you haven't really had any quality time out since leaving the hospital. I thought it'd be fun to hit up a park or something," Faith says.

"I'd like that," I say.

"But now there's not enough time because you have to fly out," she says, disappointed in the day's events.

"I can do CityWalk or Springs if that's okay," I offer up.

She smiles a bit, seeming unexpectedly happy that I want to spend time with her. So, we head on out before the flight.

She decides to stop at the Springs, an incredible outdoor shopping extravaganza with House of Blues at one end and a mix of mouse-themed and other brand stores throughout the rest. Not to forget the plethora of restaurants littered throughout. The slight Florida wind adds a pleasant coolness to the little time we have here. Ambiance aside, it's nice to be out and about with Faith.

I slow down a little as she walks, so I can watch her. Her eye was caught by a window display. Her faded jeans and fitted grey shirt with black lace print are perfect complements to the determination in her walk. She is exactly where I want to be if it weren't for having to fly to New York. At least now I know what I'll be returning to.

We spend the next few hours window-shopping and watching people walk through life. Our conversation is quaint and light, nothing clouded with past memories or future possibilities. I think she needed an evening out to just live in the moment without having to ponder the difficult decisions of life. Just enjoying the moments of our outing for what they are. It is comfortable, and I feel content.

On our way to the airport, the light air of the evening starts to weigh down a little more. A fog begins to settle on our otherwise clear venture.

"One week, huh?" she says, as the fog on our evening settles in a bit more.

"Give or take. I have to negotiate the deal. Layout the terms of royalties, etc., etc.," I attempt to summarize.

She gives me a look. It's the same look I saw in her eyes when she was talking to me at Taps & Corks. A look that says she feels like she's about to travel back down an old, familiar road she'd rather not travel.

"Just business. Nothing more," I say, leaving it short.

I can understand the lack of trust, sudden onset as it seems. It's not like our past is filled with moments that instill a sense of calm and serenity in either of us. Faith senses in me the need to not kick the sleeping dog—as much as she wants to, she leaves it alone.

"I have a few doctor's appointments while you're gone. Nothing big. Just prenatal," she changes the conversation.

"Please let me know what he says," I respond.

"She," Faith throws out.

"What?" I ask.

"What she says. My doctor's a woman," Faith corrects me.

"I didn't know. After I get back, I can start coming along," I offer up. I do want to go. I don't want to fall back into our old habits of waltzing in and out of each other's lives as the mood strikes.

"Only if you want to. I can do this myself." Faith throws all confidence in me out the window.

"I want to come along. It's my baby too. I'd like to be there, alongside you," I respond, hoping she can get her self-assurance back.

"Thanks" is all she says back. I think a part of her knows she came unhinged for a split second and is now keeping her head low.

The things the universe throws at us are never easy. It's never an overnight success without the years of struggle that lead up to it. It's never like getting back together, trying again, giving it a second chance, whatever you call it, is as simple as an unchanged replay of the first run, hoping for a different ending. It's years of gained life experiences mixed with changes in who we are versus who we were, all being paired against the other half of the second chance. It's hard and never easy, but that's the universe throwing curveballs at me while I try to make things right. But all the curveballs thrown—Viv, Jacquelyn, Ronnie, the baby—are going to make the payoff of being with Faith all the sweeter. Assuming I can leave the music behind. Assuming it all works out, and it doesn't self-destruct.

A short plane ride later, I land at JFK. Waiting for me curbside at the airport is Viv. No Logan, no Jeanine, no Spear Fist. Just Viv. The look on her face immediately turns to relief as her eyes connect with mine. The visible worry and anxiety drain from her face with a smile. I return her wave with a nod and a wink.

I honestly didn't think I'd be back in New York so soon after leaving. Hell, I didn't know if I'd ever be back. No real thoughts on the subject, but here I am, breathing in the familiar smells of my time spent here and trying to remember the good from the bad, like an old friend trying to rehash the past while sharing a lager at the local dive bar. This is no time to get whimsy and reminiscent. We have goals to accomplish and deals to make. I toss my luggage in the backseat of her rental car and ride shotgun.

Viv takes me through the streets, avoiding the parkway. I'm not paying much attention, so I'm not exactly sure where, but at least I'm not driving.

"So, when's the meeting?" I ask, trying to get straight to business.

"They weren't sure when you'd make it, so they set aside a few times over the next few days. I'll take care of setting up the time. Let's just relax for the night. I know a good place," she assures.

I look out the window at cars driving by and the buildings we pass. There is an uneasy feeling clawing at me as I look around the city I once called home, a notion whispering in my ear that I don't belong here.

Not anymore. For now, though, I must be here if only to settle my affairs.

Before too long, Viv pulls into a parking lot. It's a familiar sight, though I can't place it; perhaps it is just passing déjà vu. As we enter the watering hole, the familiarity hits me. We stopped in Queens. Last time I was at this bar, I was three sheets to the wind, laying against the kickplate on the bar, screaming along with Andrew W.K.'s "I Love New York City." Ah, old memories do haunt us at peculiar times.

We cop-a-squat at the barstools. Viv holds up two fingers, and the bartender gives her a nod. It seems that she's been here more than a few times on this leg of their tour.

"How much longer you got?" the bartender shouts over the music.

"Couple o' days. Then onto the Midwest. Chi-town, Twin Cities, St. Louis, and a few more," Viv says with a smile. It seems that she has found something to smile about.

"How's Logan?" I ask out of both personal and professional curiosity.

"Nice small talk we're starting off with here," Viv laughs back. "Logan's fine. Chilling with the band before their show."

"It's already getting up there in time. Don't you need to be there?" I inquire.

"Eventually. Wanted a quick drink first," Viv says as the bartender places our drinks in front of us.

The music of the bar provides a pleasing ambiance to the night. The unique sounds of Volbeat's "The Devil's Bleeding Crown" soothe the nerves of the coming meeting. The night couldn't be going any smoother.

"Finn!" a voice shouts.

I turn to see her. The sound of the voice is accompanied by he-who-almost-pounded-me-into-oblivion-not-once-but-twice. Of all the gin joints in all The Big Apple, they walk in here. Patrick and Katy. At least the big smile on his face is a nice change of pace.

Katy waves at me as they spring on over to us. Viv tosses me a curious look that I smile at.

I whisper to Viv, "Old friends."

She whispers back, "Moreso her than him, I presume."

But it isn't Katy to shake my hand first. Patrick, dressed in clothes that hide his skull-crushing, almost surfer-dude physique, extends a hand. As I return the shake, he wraps his free arm around me. The hug, while meaning well, presses on all the wrong spots of my bones. A need for pills whispers in my ears, but the pills are packed away in my luggage. For now, alcohol will have to dampen the pain.

"Long time no see," Patrick says with a chipper sound in his voice. "Thank you for everything."

"How're the feet? Healed up all right?" I refer to our last encounter.

"A few days of limping but nothing bad. Worst of it was the face. And the swallowed pride." Patrick smiles. "Sorry about that."

"Completely understandable. I woulda done the same thing if I was in your shoes." I smile.

Katy decides to join in. "Nice to see you, Finn. Who's this lovely lady?" she says with an elbow nudge and a wink.

"Katy, Vivian. Vivian, Katy. She's taken over the tour while I was in the hospital. I'm just here to tie things up," I answer.

"Viv. Just Viv. Nice to meet you, Katy," Viv jumps in. "How do you know Finn?"

"He saved our relationship," Katy beams.

Even Patrick is nodding his head. "It's true. Finn may be a lot of things to a lot of people. But he always does the right thing."

Viv gives me an amused nod before turning to Katy. "That he does. And it sounds like a story I need to hear."

"Funny story, but before I tell ya . . . hospitalized?" Katy changes the subject.

"Bachelor party, a little alcohol, stormy night, and a multi-car pileup," I summarize.

"Doesn't sound good," Patrick says.

"Wasn't as good for the passenger in my car." I carry a tone in my voice that answers the next unasked question.

"So sorry, sir," Patrick says, ending the topic.

They both sit next to us at the bar and order a drink. We spend a short while chatting up and small talking about Spear Fist and making a call to put them on the list for tonight's show. It's nice to sit and relax, sharing a drink with no drama. No hidden agendas to bring up at an opportune time. No ulterior motives to guide our actions. Just old friends making new friends.

"So," Viv chimes in, "Finn is a relationship savior? How did he pull that off?"

Patrick finishes a sip of his bottled beer while raising his other hand. "By helping me after I almost pummeled him to death," he says, wiping beer foam off his chin.

Viv looks to me for confirmation.

"It's true," I say. "Mistaken case of wrong place, wrong time. But in Patrick's defense, the presumption wasn't unwarranted."

Katy pipes up with a finger wave for another round. "I walked into some misguided shenanigans, but Pat and I talked."

"Talked?" I raise a brow.

Patrick sets down the empty bottle and starts his second beer. "Seriously. After you helped me back up, I sat in the elevator, riding back, just thinking. Thinking about why I acted like I did and why you did for me what you did. I knew both our actions were because of this girl." He wraps his arm around her, bringing her in for a quick hug. "We talked about everything. All our mistakes. All the reasons we did what we did. And it was great."

Katy takes the proverbial mic. "It's true. Ever since that day, things have been great. And we have you to thank."

I nod in appreciation for their kind words. "I was just a catalyst. You already had a boiling pot. Just needed things stirred the right way," I add.

Things are nice. We sit and finish our second rounds while laughing and making jokes on my behalf, all of which are well deserved.

I feel a sense of serenity because despite all my actions and childish behavior, something good came out of the incident. Which I guess is why we repaid them with the backstage access at the show, a show which is going as well as can be expected.

The night itself is going better than I hoped. No complaints from former lovers. No men chasing me with baseball bats or hitting me upside the face with a hammer of a fist. Pleasant, a word generally not used to describe a heavy metal show, but pleasant the mood is.

I stand watching the show from a similar vantage point as I did at their record release. I half expect Faith to grab my hand or some cheesy notion of romanticism. But no. No fingers are gently interlaced with mine. No arms wrap around my waist or shoulder. I stand, watching them, thinking about all the events that led up to this moment.

I try to think about this life. The nights like this one and the days that lead up to these nights: the work and sacrifice, the ecstasy and the agony of it all. The life that I have created, yes, much of that was inspired by Faith. But I watch it all play out before my eyes. The culmination of everything I have worked for and done being given back to the audience, note by note and lyric by lyric. I love it all. Every moment that I remember: the good, the bad, the ugly. The nights where songs come together in such gloriousness that the excitement keeps you going for another eight hours. The days spent alone trying to remember why you wanted this life because you haven't seen friends or family for so long, your mind starts to forget what they look like. And of course, the moments where you exit from behind a bush from just having done what was done to see the love of your life cast soul-crushing judgment with only her eyes. I look at it all.

I am not sure I can leave it all behind. I cannot fathom what my life would entail without this. I guess now, because I never had to before, I need to think about how I can do this and be a father too. Be there so Faith can be a mother. Kids can be raised on the road. I am sure of it. But for some reason, Faith won't do that. She won't follow me and be with me while I do what I do so well. I can't imagine who I would be without all this. Possibly some remnant of a guy who watches old reruns of a television show while keeping an eye on the baby so his wife can cook a meal or take a bath or whatever.

All those thoughts play so fast that my mind can't focus on any one moment or any one scenario. They just get pushed aside by the never-ending deluge of new situations and thoughts constantly entering my head. It's not a bad thing. It's just that in moments like these—a crossroad if you will—your mind won't focus. To reminisce on it all is too much. So, the universe sends something your way to make you focus or, at the very least, stop the flood of thoughts and memories.

A tap on my shoulder is what pulls me up from under the current. I turn, expecting to see a fan around my age with upturned lips, ready to tell me of his or her love for my work. Some sort of single-serving compliment to carry me through to the next one, but it is not. No. It is not some simple gesture that will be forgotten by me long before the encounter will ever leave the person's mind. Such a simple meeting would be welcome. Instead, I turn to see an expectant, smiling face. The face, though, that is the surprise.

"Funny seeing you here, Finn." Jacquelyn smirks as she sips her beer.

Jacquelyn. I am not sure what to think. Faith said they talked. Faith said Jacquelyn understood. Or did she say that? My mind has been in a constant state of low-lying fog since waking up in the hospital. But I guess the bigger preponderance at the moment is finding out why the hell she is in New York.

I shake the thoughts from my mind. "How are you?"

She extends an arm, her upturned eyebrow questioning if a hug is appropriate. I move in and wrap my arms around her. It is nice to see her, after all. She holds me close for a moment. The feeling of her pressed against me isn't as unwelcome as I suppose it should be. But comfortable places are comforting.

"I wanted to come see you in the hospital," she whispers in my ear. "Faith didn't think that would be such a good idea. Baby and all."

I give her a tighter squeeze before pulling back. "Sorry I never made it back to the bachelor party. I didn't plan on leaving you like that."

"But you did plan on leaving me?" She scratches her cheek.

I shake my head. "I meant, I wasn't going to leave things like that. Stripping, dancing, whatever, just took a moment to digest. I'm sorry I reacted the way I did."

"I think it's all water under the bridge now." She smiles.

Jacquelyn stands for a moment, peering into my eyes. I don't know if she is looking for something in them or just seeing if I am still me. She shifts her gaze to the stage.

"How were you going to leave things? Ya know, had the whole crash not happened?" She continues to stare at the stage.

There's a part of me that understands why she is staring at the stage and not at me. I know it is for the same reason that I can't look at her right now. If we were to look at each other, it might change what we want to say. Damn. What the hell is she doing in New York?

"You're a little far from home." I don't respond to her question yet. I still have to figure out what I would have said.

She turns back to me, sipping her drink. "Needed a little break, and I heard this great band was on tour. Figured I'd become a groupie or somethin'."

That might have been a guarded response, but after everything, I can understand it.

"I was falling hard for you, ya know," I say, a little under my breath.

"I know," she says, taking in a quick breath.

Apparently, it wasn't under my breath enough.

"I was all in for you. It was why I was hesitant to tell you that I danced," Jacquelyn continues. She turns back to the show. "So, you're giving all of this up for her?"

There are the words. Spoken. Pointed. Sharp. And they cut deep.

"It would seem that way." I run my hand through my hair.

"You don't have to. It's your choice." Jacquelyn's eyes are still glued to the stage.

"I don't think it's that simple anymore. Unborn and all," I gently remind her.

"Sure. But this is your life. This is what you are. The music, the stage, the venues, the road. Are you ready to give that all up for her? Your child can travel. You can have both." Jacquelyn has become a devil on my shoulder. But she might be the angel. Hell, I am not sure anymore.

"Faith," I start to say.

"Oh, I know. Faith told me all about you two. Who you guys were back in the day. How it all was before the fame. How she followed your colorful career from afar, reading about your exploits while standing in line at the grocery store or some street-side magazine stand. She told me about her and you and Ronnie. The torch you still hold for her and her for you, apparently. I know the tumultuous tale of torrid trysts." She suddenly stops as if I was cued to interrupt.

"So…" I urge her to continue.

"So, she's not the only one who carries a torch for you. If I am to be honest, I don't think she's the only one your torch holds a flame for." She steps closer to me.

Her eyes dive deep into mine. Our breath is soft. The feel of the bass pounding through the concrete floors seems to slide us closer and closer. Our lips hover just out of reach.

"You don't have to decide anything tonight, Finn. I wouldn't do that to you. But I won't wait forever. I'm not a consolation prize," she whispers in a tone that is somehow both sexy as hell and stern to the point of making me feel ashamed, a little aroused, and a little ashamed for feeling aroused. I think this might be the first time in my life I'll take the shame over the sex.

She leans in, planting a kiss on my cheek. "I'll see you soon. Don't be a stranger. You still have my number."

She leaves it at that, walking away. My mind is spinning—spiraling out of control and plummeting toward Earth. All I can think is that a pill sounds good right now. I thought I was somehow passed all the temptation, passed all the choices being thrown at me like I am some sort of sacred prize for someone. I am not. And no matter, no woman deserves to be a consolation prize for someone else.

I reach down for my pills, and the bottle rises with one last reprieve. Damn. One pill. It makes me wonder how many I have been taking and how often. I thought I had a relatively full bottle when I flew up here. No matter now, though. The bottle gives me one last dose to ease the pain.

Further downward my spiral plummets, though a little slower toward the ground below. Faith and my baby trying to catch me. Jacquelyn and the life that I love trying to shove Faith out of the way in some attempt to be my salvation. These strange thoughts fill my head without any semblance of organization. I want Faith. I've always wanted Faith. The honest truth of the matter is it never would have worked out between Jacquelyn and me. To make it as simple as possible, it wasn't in the cards. Perhaps she just never saw that. Maybe I am wrong. What she does present is an alternative. A chance to have Faith and the life that I love. A life that Faith has only witnessed from a safe distance—cities or countries away. A life that has given Faith pause on giving me a second chance, but a life that is misunderstood by those not directly in it.

I guess now I must deal with Jacquelyn and whatever emotions and unfinished business still lingers in the universe.

"It's funny that you like these weird places to watch the show," Viv shouts as she hands me a beer.

I take a sip in hopes that it can ease the pain, both emotional and physical, that I feel. One pill just doesn't take the edge off like it first did.

"It's peaceful back here." I sip again.

"But the party is down there. Hell, you're farther away than anyone in the seats," Viv says, grabbing my hand, leading me away.

"The distance gives me a viewpoint to take it all in. A place to reflect on things." I offer up a rare dose of honest vulnerability.

"I saw what happened, Finn." She lets go of my hand now that she knows I am following.

"You have to narrow that down a bit," I joke.

"You and Jacquelyn. I saw her." Viv's tone isn't even subtly leading. It's in my face pointing it out with half of a smile on her lips.

"We were talking. Jacquelyn never came to visit me, ya know." I sip my beer.

"She never came because Faith told her not to. Faith needs you, now more than ever. At least that's what I'm told," Viv offers up.

We walk for a few moments, listening to D.B. interact with the audience—some shit about being in New York and how great they all are.

Viv slows her pace. "You're a regular 'Mr. Self Destruct'."

"Is that what the long silence was for? To think of a Nine Inch Nails song title?" I chuckle.

"Yes. No." Viv scrunches her nose. "It's true, though. The name fits. We could have had something."

Viv turns to me and looks me dead in the eye. She doesn't move closer, keeping her distance as she stares. It's weird. I can see in her eyes that there's no lingering emotion, unlike with Jacquelyn. Hell, Jacquelyn told me I had options. With Viv, though, it's matter of fact. She looks at me and our past. She stares at what could have been without the yearning to try and rekindle it.

I am impressed with her state of mind and slightly jealous that I've never been that guy, never been one to let smoldering fires die out. I always have to suck the last bit of life from each and every ember.

"But you're with Logan." I test the waters to make sure my assumption is correct.

She shakes her head and laughs at me. "Not what I was implying. You cared for all of us, and I'm betting that you cared, on some level, for every woman you've ever been with."

She flashes her all-access pass to a couple of security guards so they'll let us pass. The old familiar halls of the backstage area. The grit and dirt that makes the magic happen all hidden back here.

"I like to think so," I say with a hint of uncertainty to her end.

"And I bet that every single one of those women, or at least a good number of them, could have ended up as a long term, or a permanent relationship, had you not been stuck on Faith." She finger-jabs me with the last of her words.

"Not at all. You left me. . . remember you said one day you'd tell the story of us? 'The great Fairlane Incidents' as I believe you called them." I chuckle. "And Jacquelyn was ended by Faith and other circumstances."

"And what about every other girl before us? What about Jacquelyn? What are those 'other circumstances' you mention?" She stops walking as she opens the backstage green room door. "Do you ever wonder why all your relationships have failed? Why they keep collapsing on themselves?"

The room is a little quieter than the halls once the door closes behind us. The inside is simple with two couches and a coffee table topped with finger food and sweets. A fridge off in the corner is stocked with an assortment of beer, malt beverages, and sodas. Engaged in conversation are Jeanine and Logan. The rest of Logan's bandmates are huddled in the far corner, beer bottles in hand, laughing over something they find amusing.

"There are moments I've tried to answer that for myself, but I only come to one conclusion: right place, wrong time." I grab a fresh beer from the fridge.

I twist the cap as Viv motions Logan over. Jeanine decides to join in the conversational fun. My defenses want to go up like some sort of force field around the Starship Enterprise. The sight of Jeanine and what she blew up barside makes me feel a little tight, but she is here. She is hundreds of miles from her home, far from any comfort she knows. Yes, she did it for her husband, to make sure his success wasn't entirely dependent on my lack of any sort of contingency plan in case I was injured. She also did it for me, and for that, I keep my guard down.

Logan shoots out her hand and gives me a hearty shake. Her freshly dyed pink hair is much less tweaker than when I first discovered her. Even the style is not as hectic and disheveled.

Before Logan can say anything, Jeanine grabs me and wraps her arms around me. "It's nice to see you."

Kind words are hard to digest sometimes. The feeling that everything you just felt a moment ago was wrong puts a whisper in my mind that I'm a jerk for feeling that way. So, I respond with the only thing I can think of. "I'm sorry I missed your wedding."

Jeanine shakes her head and gives me a sad smile. "We're all just glad you are okay." She turns to Viv, who is whispering something to Logan, "So, what has he done now?" Jeanine jabs at me playfully.

"We were just talking about him and his great ability to self-destruct his relationships," Viv fills them in.

As if rehearsed in some off, off, off-Broadway production of "The Finn Fairlane Story," Logan and Jeanine both nod their heads with a thesaurus of confirmations to Viv's statement. The almost-forced laughter, while trying not to hurt my fragile ego, comes across like they rehearsed this very moment in some sort of elaborate and slightly cruel prank. Except they didn't. It was organic, a real moment where two people's gut reactions about me confirmed the third person's—that I self-destruct. Now, as much as I would love to move the conversation onto a new subject, something a little less about me and more about anything else in the universe, I have a feeling that is not going to happen. What I am about to be part of is the education of Finn Fairlane and everything I have done, why I made those decisions, and what I should be doing about it all.

"Now I know that you and I don't fuckin' talk outside of music and tour shit, but I do talk with my lovely girl." Logan starts the class for me. "From what it sounds like, I might be way fuckin' off base here, but it sounds like you can't let go. Don't get me wrong; it's not a bad fuckin' thing. Your inability to let go, hold onto whatever it is that lingers inside your brain, is what spawned the music, the career that was fuckin' Finn Fairlane."

I nod my head. "I think that's pretty well established."

Logan huffs and nods in agreement. "Then why can't you fill in the blanks, the space between then and now?"

Jeanine raises her hand slightly, as if to politely interject. "It's what happened back then. The romanticization of what could have been. Of what you wanted it to be. All she did was solidify the end to you and her long after it had already expired. You may have gone on to bigger things, venues, tours, foreign countries, but your heart and your mind are still on campus back in freshman year."

Wow. I'd say from the mouths of babes but a child she is anything but anymore. Once again, she has proven herself to me. I am glad that this time, at least, she is on my side. At least I think they are all on my side, just trying to help me along this path we call life.

Viv turns to Logan with an apology in her eye. "I hate to bring this up, but it's to the point."

Logan nods. "Baby, you ain't the first to play in my sandbox, and I ain't the first to play in yours."

"Sandbox?" I joke. "Kinda a dry place. I would've gone with 'splash in your pool,' 'wade in your waters,' something with a little more moisture."

Logan chuckles. "You've only ever played in them during rainy season."

I nod, smile, and turn to Viv.

Viv smiles as she shakes her head. "Even as I was looking you in the eye, balls deep on your dick, I saw it in your eyes. Of course, at that moment, I didn't know what to think. I thought maybe it was me. I wasn't doing something right; you weren't enjoying it."

I throw up a hand. "Oh no. You were . . . wonderful."

"No need to play coy around me, Finn," Jeanine interjects. "I've been privy to your illustrious escapades for a while now."

"Just trying to show some couth," I defend.

"Even I know it's a little too late for that shit," Logan tosses in her two cents.

"Back to my point." Viv gets her floor back. "I saw it then. Only now I know what it was. It wasn't some unknown greatness floating through your head. It wasn't some moment of musing that you'll write about in some future song. It was thoughts of Faith.

Thoughts of a long passed 'what if.' Had that little notion not been biting the back of your mind, some constant reminder throughout the years of what you once had, who knows what you could have had? What we could have had."

Logan tilts her head toward Viv, a gesture not unnoticed by Viv. "Not that I'm complaining. I quite like where the adventure led me. I'm just saying that, present circumstances unknown, it could have been something."

I chuckle. "No need to worry, Logan. She has no residual embers still clinging to life and smoldering for me. Her fire for me has died and been reignited in a luminescent lesbian flame for you."

All of their heads turn to me. Viv says what they are all thinking, "Luminescent lesbian flame?"

I shrug my shoulders. "I wanted something colorful."

"You're an ass, Finn," Logan spits out with a chuckle.

"That I may be. But I'm the reason this night exists. So, ass or not, you all are glad I'm around," I respond with a little unintended narcissism. "But where it led was worth it all, was it not?"

Viv looks into Logan's eyes, a gesture the defensive Logan is not used to. Her shifting posture broadcasts it for all to see. "Of course, it was. No offense, Finn. But this is where I belong. So for me, yes. But have you ever asked yourself that question?"

And immediately, as if the uncomfortableness that Logan felt was cued to jump into me, I start smiling that unsure smile. The smile of a child caught with his hand in the cookie jar. The swaying back and forth, shuffling my feet as my body is attacked by those words, words that I guess I never have faced myself, no matter how many times I thought I have.

Viv continues her inquisition. "I mean that Katy girl seemed to be all hunky-dory with her boy, but what if you were that guy? Hell, we had a great time together, and from what I can tell, I made you happy."

I nod at her words.

"Even Jaquelyn seemed to make you happy. You had no reason to stop seeing her. It's not like she's the first girl you ever saw pick up a dollar bill with her lady parts," Viv continues.

Again, I throw my hands up. "Why does the bill keep getting smaller? It was a twenty."

"Not the point, Finn," Viv continues. "The point is, is that any of those girls, and I'm sure there were a few more between, you could have had a successful future with. A girl who was a clean slate. Someone who you didn't have a checkered past with and old preconceptions wouldn't weigh into every decision."

"I'm losing focus," I admit. "What's the point?"

"Why Faith? Why throw all those things out the window? Why self-destruct every good possibility that has come your way since the day you two finally went your separate ways?" Viv's words hit me hard.

Have I ever actually given any thought to those words? I have in that stupid coffeehouse, existentialism way, pondering the greater meaning of life, love, loss, and the purposelessness of it all. Or whatever college-age bullshit I deluded myself with to try and move forward while really just running on a metaphorical treadmill. I mean, you turn it on, the ground below you moves, the digital readout says that you've been running for forty-five minutes, and you've run four miles. The thing is, though, you haven't. You step off the platform and you are right where you began. You haven't moved in any sort of way that anyone can see. Sure, you're out of breath, and your clothes are soaked with sweat, but you are in the same exact spot you were in forty-five minutes ago. You are in the same exact spot you've been for the last forty-five minutes.

You were running in place. That's all I've been doing. It gives you a workout, sure. I'm not saying it doesn't. But exercise aside, we've stood still. Mentally, I've been standing still, too scared to move on and too afraid to make anything real. I am not sure if it was because I was too frightened to let go of Faith or some other reason. Perhaps I was too afraid to repeat the same mistakes. The irony of it all is that my own fears caused me to repeat the same mistakes over and over again, time after time.

I look up to see Jeanine texting on her phone while trying to hold in a smile.

"Everything all right?" I ask her.

"Just telling sis about all the fun she's missing right now." Jeanine laughs.

"Thanks. Glad we can get more people in on this. I think after all this, I'm going to go get some sleep. You kids enjoy yourselves." I turn to leave and wave bye to them.

As I exit the door, Viv squeezes through before it closes. "I'll walk you to your hotel."

"I still have to find one," I say a bit sheepishly.

"You bought a plane ticket but didn't make a hotel reservation? Dumbass," she playfully scolds.

"Had other things on my mind." I shrug.

"I bet. You can crash with us," Viv says, as if there is no other acceptable option. "Let's grab your bag from my car for the just in case."

The walk is quiet for a minute or two, just two friends keeping each other company. There is a feeling of unease that crawls around my skin, like little spiders gently tiptoeing over my body hairs. They try not to disturb me, but I can feel them all. The unease of it is my fault, I think. Perhaps all the events in my life that have led up to this moment are my fault. Not my doing. Not some grand cosmic plan. Just my fault, like a series of crappy events that all led to here. It has to be this new understanding that I have been scared of. Otherwise, it wouldn't bother me so.

"Sorry if that was too uncomfortable back there." Viv breaks the silence.

"Wasn't your fault. Just brought up some long-needed realizations," I start. "I should probably be thanking you."

Viv lets out a laugh. We both take a few steps, breathing in the night air. I take a look around the Big Apple and think about how it differs from The City Beautiful. There's nothing here to steal you away from your adulthood. Nothing here to make you grab for your lost childhood. Just the living entity that is New York, the nightlife that breathes soul into the morning that resuscitates the night. The never-ending cycle that is New York. And it is wonderful. Nothing jaded. Nothing to make you believe in fairy tales. Just unre-strained, in-your-face-city life from the most brutally honest group of tell-it-like-it-is people—New Yorkers.

A few more steps of our ten block journey stops us at a red light, waiting to cross to the hotel. Viv turns to me. "There was a part of me that wanted to say, 'I can think of a way to thank me.'"

I let out a short laugh as I look toward the night sky.

"I just didn't want you to take me too seriously," she amends her statement.

"I wouldn't have thought you were. Even if I did, Logan kinda scares me, ya know," I offer up.

"She has a defensive side to her. I'll give her that," Viv responds.

"Don't let that scare you off. She's loyal. Guarded."

We both cross as the light turns green. The night air stays welcoming as we enter the lobby to what is now my hotel.

"What about Faith?" Viv asks.

"What about her?" I say, pushing the elevator button.

"I made a joke about you and me. You said Logan scared you off. So, what about Faith?" Viv asks for clarity on the subject.

"Faith. If there ever was such a sweet subject." I let it trail off while I think of the answer. As the elevator dings to open its doors, the answer chimes in my head. "She wants me to leave this all behind."

Viv lets out a laugh loud enough to turn a few random heads. "Yeah, like that'll happen." But the look in my eyes as I turn to her cuts her laughter short. "You can't be serious?"

I shrug my shoulders. "Why not? I've had a good run."

"And you're still running. You are still in the game. You are still great," Viv defends. "Why cash in your chips while you're still hot?"

I laugh. "Hot? I haven't been hot for a long time. Warm, sure. But the days of rock 'n roll like I knew are long over. The sad reality is my time in the limelight ended long ago. Now I'm just living on borrowed time, hoping to make one last great hit and cash it all in, again."

"So, that's it?" Viv scorns. "What about Spear Fist? What about Logan Square? What about all the people, like me and Jeanine, who actually enjoy you being who you are?"

"There's the rub." I tap the side of my nose. "The proverbial what-to-do."

The elevator doors open, and the walk to her room is drowned in silence.

We do find an amicable middle ground to comfortably relax in, laughing as we talk and pass the time till sleep sets in.

The funny thing is that Viv and I had great sexual chemistry, but Logan's disclaimer sounds in my head—innies, not outies. So, the night ends without any sexual escapades or events that will lead to an awkward next day, which just leaves the meeting with the record company.

CHAPTER 6

The Impression that I Get

The meeting room is pretty nondescript. The table is your typical laminate office table with a hole in the middle for phone cords and such, and a few generic-looking, black cloth office chairs so we can stare at each other while figuring out the details of the contract. At least the floor-to-ceiling windows overlook the Big Apple. It's a beautiful sight to see the hustle and bustle of the tiny cars and even tinier people below, all moving about their day, trying to make deals, deadlines, and whatever else the city needs from them.

But the executives don't seem to want to stare at the life below us. The suits they wear mean business while my jeans, T-shirt, and suit coat give mixed signals. But here we all are. Even Viv is more professionally dressed than I am. But it's me they want, so it's me they get.

The thought of the push and pull of the contracts, wheeling and dealing to make things happen, starts to irk me. The gnawing sensation of being told counter-offers just to land where I know we are going to land eats away at my bones—my finally healing bones. But now they are starting to hurt. I pull out a bottle of pain-killers (or muscle relaxers, or whatever remnants of prescription and over-the-counter drugs happen to be left) from my front right pocket and dump a couple into my hand. A quick look to make sure there aren't too many (though the number for too many has changed recently), and then I toss them in my mouth. A quick head tilt back, dry gulp down, and I turn back to the record execs.

"So? I had to come up here?" I start.

"Spear Fist is yours, are they not?" one of them says.

"Sure. But they are hers too. Viv took over the tour after my accident," I tell them. They should know this. They do their research. I am not sure what game they are playing here.

Ah, the games, the subtle push and pull of words designed to try and get you to give up as many of your rights to the music as they can get without you realizing it. I've done this for far too long to play this game over and over, but over and over is how the game is played.

In all honesty, the meeting is the last thing on my mind. Even as I sit here at the table with the execs and Viv, my mind is thinking about New York. It is thinking about the life I left behind to move south, just to end up here tonight. I remember the radio commercials and taxicab advertisements that whispered to me. I remember why I moved. I remember wanting to get away from moments like this, not the meetings and making futures happen. That's part of the business. It's the game of the business. I wanted to get away from the young bucks. The new adults fresh out of school that happened to be in some position of limited power, even though if you sniffed hard enough, you could still smell dorm room sex on them. They are the hotshots who think that because they remember sixty percent of the crap they read about while getting their bachelors and have minimal field experience, they know it all. It's that position of naive arrogance that I wanted to get away from—that I was tired of dealing with. But here I am, sitting with two guys who are precisely that.

What I'd rather be doing is wandering the city. I'd preferably be visiting the places I left behind: a stroll past my old apartment building; a walk past my favorite restaurants or a chat with the bartender I used to know, assuming they are still there. I'd sooner be talking with Faith about this bullshit I have to do right now. I'd rather be chatting with Jaquelyn about the future we could have had if only the car didn't smash into me and kill my girl's ex-fiancé. (That's a lot to chew on right now.) But no, I am here and about to hear something stupid come out of one of the guys' mouths.

"But you are the man in charge," the other one says, as if to remind me of my place in all this. As if I will jump up, shove Viv aside and declare that, yes, I am the man in charge. Screw him.

"I don't think my penis has much to do with my authority," I joke.

They turn to each other and pull their papers close to them. The first one turns to me. "We don't have to do this if you can't be civil."

"You wanted to meet with me. Viv could have handled it, but you wanted me. I told her no. She nudged and insisted until she got me here. So far, I'm more impressed with her abilities than yours," I say to them.

Why do I say such harsh words to two guys that can offer me lots of money? Cause I don't care about them. I don't give a crap about their student loans or their car repairs. I care about Spear Fist, Viv, and about my future. If I show them I care about them, then it gives them the upper hand.

The one I seemingly offended more stands up and looks toward the door before glancing down at his colleague. The two don't say anything. I can sense Viv's eyes locked on me, trying to telepathically call me to her. She wants to see my eyes. She wants to know I am not going to fuck this up. The irony here is that if I turn to her, I will. So, I don't.

The second pushes his chair back from the table. He rises without looking at me. A wise move. Show me you don't care. The first guy, though, he glances at me, and I can see his fear.

"That's fine. Your bosses won't care that you lost Spear Fist. There are others out there," I start as they take a step toward the door. "But how are your bosses going to take it when you tell them that you mucked up a deal with Finn Fairlane?" I wait for a reaction as they continue to the door. A hand reaches the handle. "That Finn Fairlane won't deal now or any time in the future with them because you decided to walk away?"

The handle does not turn. The first one glances back at the other. Some silent conversation plays out, and though I have no clue what they are saying, I know they are both realizing that scare tactics don't work on me. "Walk away if you want. I can call your boss right now. He'll be happy to hear from me. How happy will he be to hear from you?"

They sigh simultaneously, both returning to their seats.

"Fine," one of the suits says. "Let's move on."

They start to explain their want for Spear Fist, their desire to have them on their label. They both spout the same crap I've heard time and time again about where they see the band going and all the same scripted bull they've spewed before. They have their usual demands, which will be whittled down considerably by the time I am through, but my pills kick in and kick in hard. Did I take any right before the meeting? I don't remember. I may have. I must have. My wandering mind only does this when the pills are making my pain go away. And the more pills, the less pain.

I try to stay focused on their words. I want to make sure that anything I respond to isn't giving away any of our rights. I want to respond appropriately, not because I give a crap if they know I am stoned on some pills right now but because they will exploit the fact I am high right now. A mistake that has cost many dearly.

I don't know how long I was lost in my thoughts. It only seemed like a few seconds. I think I only said a few words to myself, but I hear them repeat my name.

"Finn? Finn?" the second suit says.

I look up at them. I didn't even realize I was staring down. I quickly rub my left temple and wince in feigned pain.

"Excuse me, I need to step out for a moment," I say, rising from my seat.

One of the suits speaks up. "Um, we have to get through this. We were in the middle of something."

I turn to him. "And I'll be back shortly. It's not the end of the world. Talk with Viv while I'm out. Order some pies, pepperoni and sausage. Just give me a minute to take a leak."

I exit the meeting and walk to the bathroom. Surprisingly enough, I find myself actually needing to take a leak, after which I find myself staring back at me in the mirror. I need to get my head in the game. I called a timeout. Never a good move to do first, but who am I kidding? These kids are new to the game and only have playbook experience and minimal field time. I don't care that I called time; Viv is still in there making sure the deal doesn't go south.

I pull out my pills to do a quick inventory count but find the well has run dry. No rattling sound as it exits my pocket. No little pill, whole, broken, smooth, or jagged to help ease the pain. I need to be able to concentrate, but it's just not happening right now.

I flip the lever up and turn on the faucet. I splash some water onto my face a few times. I know that it doesn't actually help sober you up from whatever chemicals that have taken control of your brain. It does help slap some cold sense back into me for a moment though, a quick jolt to grab my attention, and hopefully hold onto it long enough to finish this shit.

I grab a paper towel from the automated, touch-free dispenser and begin to dry my face. The door opens, and one of the suits walks in.

A self-deprecating smirk crosses his face. "You were right. A bathroom break was a good idea."

"Sometimes I have good ideas," I joke. "I'm heading back now."

"Pizza is on its way," he says, unzipping his pants.

I head back to the meeting room to find Viv sitting by herself.

"Where's the other guy?" I ask, looking around.

"They decided to take advantage of the break," she starts. "One's in the restroom; the other went looking for a vending machine for soda."

I pull out a chair and turn it toward Viv as I take a seat.

"You've done an impeccable job with the tour, handling the band, and everything that I was supposed to be doing," I begin, making sure I have her attention.

"Thanks?" she says, raising a brow. "I had help."

I nod in acknowledgment. "I know. But you have been the front of it all."

Her attention is still locked fully on me, waiting to see where the ship is headed.

"You have been able to pull this off with just my notes and a love for the music. Is this something that interests you?" I ask.

"What?" Viv asks, the confusion evident on her face.

"What we are doing now—meetings, tours, life on the killing road. Is this something that interests you?" I continue.

"I guess, but I don't know what I am doing. I still feel like I need a crutch or training wheels or whatever. This is like brand fuckin' new, Finn." The hysteria in her voice grows as the realization of where the ship is heading becomes clearer.

"I know. I'm here. But you're at the helm now," I start.

She interrupts with a hint of panic, "Why now, all of a sudden?"

"It's time for something new. The whole reason I left New York was to get away from meetings like this." I pause as I look around the meeting room. I walk to the window and look down at the ground. The cars zooming about on the street below in anonymity make me almost happy to be here. I find a strange comfort in the overwhelming size of this city. "I love this life. I love the music. I love it all. I am just done. There is something in me that is ready for something new."

Viv looks at me, searching for what that "something new" is. "Is that something new Faith or Jacquelyn?"

I turn to her with an unsure look in my eye. She knows that is the answer I am searching for.

"My waters run much deeper than just Faith or Jacquelyn. I'm not sure I can even express the thoughts running in my head right now," I admit as I walk away from the window.

"Try me." She smiles.

Before I can even attempt an explanation, our conversation is interrupted by the opening door and the suits returning with sodas for us all.

They both sit down at the table. "So, Finn, we were about to discuss where we see Spear Fist heading."

"Yes, you were," I butt in. "When I stepped away, I realized something."

The suits look at each other before looking back at me.

"What is that?" one of them replies.

"You asked for me by name," I begin.

"That is correct," the suit confirms.

"Your label knew I was out of commission. It's why they sent you and not someone with more experience. It's why, even after I am sure Vivian explained my situation, you demanded to have me here," I continue.

As I continue, I see the sweat start to build on their foreheads. I can see the nervousness grow as each word exits my mouth. To them, this meeting is as much about landing a deal for themselves as it is meeting me. Fanboying out is not professional and not part of the agreement.

"Viv works for me. I run Fairlane Records, and she is my proxy. You are her account," I ad-lib.

"Fairlane Records? We were unaware you started your own label," the suit says, his nervousness growing more and more.

"The details are being hammered out," I continue to bullshit them. "I started it while I've been recovering. Viv and her team have been more than sufficient in handling my affairs." Luckily Viv is smart enough not to say anything and go with the flow.

"We understand," the other suit interjects.

"And as you understand, Viv is who you will be addressing for the rest of this meeting. Not me. I am invisible. Deaf, though, I am not."

I watch the gears turn in their minds. Each of the suits wonders how they are going to handle Viv. I can see the silent conversation between the two of them as they figure out how to handle this change. My words continue to echo loudly in their heads, "deaf, though, I am not."

I roll back in my chair and stare out the window toward the Big Apple, the city that made this meeting possible. Had I not worn out my welcome here, had I not needed to get away and reinvent my career, had so many little factors not fallen into place, I wouldn't be here right now. But I am here, back in the city where this chapter of my life all started.

Yes, I got picked up and noticed in Chicago. But my behind-the-music aspect of my life and career didn't start until New York. So, here I am, sitting in a meeting while facing the behemoth of a city and looking at the same sidewalks walked by Neil Diamond and Mike D, Cyndi Lauper and DMC. So many great musicians of influence beyond their years, and I am somehow a part of that. Looking out over these streets, it feels good.

I listen to Viv and the suits talk, the details of everything being hammered out. It feels nice to sit back and let the worry fall on someone else, someone who has the eager eyes of innocence and the gusto for diving into the industry. To think about how our relations started versus where they are now. I believe that sometimes the happenstance of life happens for a reason.

My ears pick up on something that is said. To be honest, I'm not sure exactly what the suit said, but I hear a pause in Viv's voice as she responds. I lean in and whisper to her, "Whatever you feel works. Go with it. Just don't sign anything until I give it a read. They are more than authorized to leave you with unsigned contracts. Nothing of importance is that imminent."

She gives me a slight nod and takes a deep breath. I can see her gather herself and regain her initial confidence. For the rest of this meeting, I sit in blissful reminiscence about my years in New York, my time before in Chicago, and the months in Florida. I trace all my moments, all my decisions, and connect the dots that ended up taking me here; it's the start, apparently, of something new—Fairlane Records, or whatever bullshit name I spewed off the cuff. The thing is, though, it worked. Whatever happened, whatever the words I said, it worked. Viv is in charge as I watch from further behind the scenes, tears welling in my eyes—a smile on my face.

I never thought that for a kid who wanted nothing more than to be on stage, soaking in the adoration of fans, that being the furthest behind the scenes possible, and still be in the scene, is where I would find happiness in it all.

At least for the moment, but tomorrow is another day.

CHAPTER 7

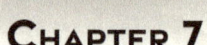

I Give As Good As I Get

The night is invigorating. The meeting went well. In some ways, it went better than I could have expected. Viv has taken the reins which my hands are tired of holding—calloused and worn thin from years of tugging and abuse. New ideas flow through my mind in waves, as broad strokes of forming plans take root. And as plans take root, they need sustenance to make sure they grow. There is no better nutrient for the seeds of music than that of alcohol. Luckily hotels have long since taken to the notion that travelers like to imbibe while away from their regular domiciles, thus I do not have far to walk. I turn down the lobby and follow the walkway to the welcoming room that has a bar and bottles upon bottles of various poisons to soothe a weary traveler. I am one such traveler.

I cop a squat center bar. Before I can even wave a finger to grab the barkeep's attention, his rag is already flung over his white button-up and black suspendered shoulder, and he is picking up a glass to pour me whatever my heart desires.

"Widow Jane, neat," I say.

Before I can even fully settle into the quiet reverie of victory, I feel a tap on my shoulder and turn to see a brunette smiling at me. The purposefully grey streak just off-center from the front of this mystery woman's forehead is an unusual choice for someone with otherwise jet-black hair. Perhaps she is a fan of the mutant comics. Her olive skin and soft, rounded facial features, accented by the dim lighting of the bar, emphasize her Far East beauty. There is a familiarity in the way she dresses—a casual uncaring coupled with a finish that is sure to turn heads.

I am not sure why this stranger is so eager to talk to a man who just sat down, but I am not one to reject such a fascinatingly beautiful woman.

"A man who knows his bourbons." She smiles, batting her eyelashes as the bartender places the bottle back on the shelf.

I give her a nod. "It goes down smooth."

I glance at the bartender as he slides the glass in front of me. He notices my eyes shift to the lady next to me; it is a subtle glance that tries to ask if she is just a lady or a lady of the night. He casually shrugs his shoulders as he shakes his head no. If he hasn't seen her here before, then odds are I won't be dealing with any sort of financial transaction, not that anything will transpire either way. I have Faith anxiously awaiting my return in Orlando.

Her look shifts. I've seen the shifting look countless times before. The look that at this moment in time—this moment in my life—is wearing thin, getting old, and becoming a bore. It's not that I don't appreciate the gesture or the meaning behind the look—the glimmer of recognition that I am someone they recognize from a magazine or television interview. I do appreciate it. It's just this night, this moment, is supposed to be mine, a moment of self-reflection for what was accomplished tonight. But privacy and moments of being alone are things that I chose to possibly forfeit long ago. So, here I sit, next to some exotic beauty who I believe is most likely not a hooker.

"I know this may sound strange," she begins (always a preface to something I've heard before). "I've heard a lot of good things about you."

"I'm sure they aren't all true." I turn to her, taking a swig of my bourbon.

She smiles and chuckles a little. "Esther." She extends her hand to me.

I set down my drink and shake her hand. "Nice to meet you."

I am not sure if it is really nice to meet her or if I am just being cordial, polite, giving an empty pleasantry to fill the moment. It doesn't really matter, I guess. Hell, the company can be a good thing.

"What's your poison?" I gesture to the bottles behind the bar.

She puts up her hand to catch the attention of the eavesdropping barkeep. "Old Grand Dad, neat."

Those words make me choke on the air. "You must have something you're trying to kill inside you."

She lets out a hearty laugh. "It was the first drink I ever had. Something about it stuck with me. It's the only whiskey I drink."

The bartender places a coaster in front of her, followed by the spirit. I motion to her glass, then to myself, and then make a writing gesture to put it on my tab. He nods and leaves.

"I hope you don't mind the company. You have a look about you..." Esther trails off.

"I do have a certain look to me, so I'm told." I'm not sure where she is going with this. Maybe it is her way of asking if she could sit. Maybe I should say she can. So, I extend a hand at the empty seat next to me.

She slides over one and turns my direction.

"Something good happened tonight. I can tell," Esther says, as if she's some sort of seer.

I sip my bourbon. "It did. Contract negotiations. Things are looking good."

"Thus, your reason for celebration." She turns to the otherwise empty bar (save one table in the corner), then back to me. "But there's no one else with you. A party of one is so lonely."

I hear it. A hint in her voice. A whisper of sensualism. I do appreciate the attention, everyone does, but I also much enjoy my time to myself so I can sort out my thoughts.

"What exactly are your intentions with me?" I bluntly get to the point. I wave to the bartender for another round as I polish off the current.

"Only the best of." She sips her drink with a little slip of her tongue. A little on the nose, but I don't think Esther beats around any sort of bush, so to speak.

"You know what they say about those kinds of intentions?" I ask, hearing the bartender laugh a muffled laugh.

"The road to hell and all. But Finn, may I call you Finn? Navigating those roads doesn't have to be all that tricky. As they say, it's about the journey, not the destination." She caresses my arm, not in an obvious way. Subtle, gently, as if she was casually moving her arm and her fingers happened to brush against me. Except it was obvious and not as delicate as she had hoped.

"It's a journey I've been on for many, many years," I begin.

"And one he's looking to end, unless I can change his mind," a third voice calls out.

I didn't hear her footsteps. I didn't detect the click-clack of her heels echoing on the marble floor. I was engaged in a conversation I've had one time too many, and yet I didn't hear them. I didn't see Esther look to her, nor did I notice her stop a few feet behind me. But the voice is undeniable. It is a voice that has confused me—that has tempted me (and won on a few occasions)—a voice that apparently is still fighting for me—Jacquelyn.

"I see you met my Esther." Jacquelyn smiles.

"He has," Esther interjects, "and everything you've told me rings true, so far."

After giving Ether a friendly hello kiss on both cheeks, Jacquelyn wraps her arms around me, regardless of whether I wanted to hug her or not.

I do reciprocate—a little out of common civility, and a little out of the joy I still get from seeing her.

There is a part of me that begins to hurt as I hold her. It's a bone-deep pain where the pain had started to recede, a pain that causes shortness of breath for a moment. I reach into my pocket, but the bottle is still empty. No magical refills have occurred since the last time I pulled it out. It looks like I'll have to grin and bear it this bout as I slip the bottle back in my pocket.

"Still on those from the accident, I see," Jacquelyn notes out loud.

"Pain is acting up. I think my years have started taking their toll on me." I shrug.

Jacquelyn opens a hand purse, clutch thingy and pulls out something. She holds it in her fingers, bringing it to my lips. "Say 'ah.'"

I open my mouth as she pops in a pill. I swallow with my bourbon (always doctor recommended) and nod a thank-you to her.

"I didn't realize you were a walking wealth of pharmaceuticals," I jest.

"I'm a lady of many talents." She winks. "Speaking of ladies of many talents, you and Esther seem to be friends."

"Only for the moment. I should be getting back to my hotel." I start to stand as I pull out my wallet.

Jacquelyn pats the seat I just rose from. "Come on, sit. It's not like you're going to just kick back watching TV in your hotel room all night. This is New York City."

I let out a forced, exaggerated, loud sigh as I resign to sitting back down. "What is on the agenda for tonight?" Yes, there is suspicion dripping off my chin in those words, but I am here, so I'll play along.

Jacquelyn gives Esther a dog-sly smile. "Whatever the mood strikes."

I down the drink in front of me. I figure either this evening is going to go exactly how I think they think it should go, and I am going to need far more mental lubrication, or it is going to need to become something I'd not remember anyway. So, either way, I'm just getting a jump on what needs to be done.

Both girls lean toward me. It's a moment that should never make a man in my shoes uncomfortable, but this moment is. Jacquelyn knows I am trying to work things out with Faith. Maybe she just doesn't realize that the drunken sexcapades with randoms are coming to an end. Then again, she might realize just that, and that is why she is doing this, one last sexcapade to send me off. I mean if that's the case, then who am I to deny someone a send-off party?

Softly breathing into each ear is Jacquelyn and Esther, a veritable global sampling of things to leave behind. Esther exhales softly in my right ear, "Are you ready for the real celebration?"

I turn to my drink. It's moved a bit from where I left it last, at least I think it did. That shouldn't even matter, though it sticks out to me for some reason. I take a big gulp. The taste is off, like the barkeep used a dirty glass and poured a different bourbon, something different that offsets the flavor just a little.

"Ladies. This isn't why I came here tonight. I was just enjoying the moment," I say.

The pain in my bones fades, as a gentle flush through me relaxes my muscles. The pain is gone. I think that pill she gave me finally set in. That was one quality pill. I feel like I could be sitting on a chaise lounge, poolside at some resort, sipping Mai Tais while sucking down shrimp cocktail. That is if I wasn't here. But damn, this calm sensation is taking over me. All the cares in my head are neatly nestled away in a dark corner to be forgotten for a while.

Jacquelyn leans in to say, "And we are here for you. We are what you really want. A reason to stay."

I can feel my brow furrow. Jacquelyn's words make sense, pointed and sharp. Mean, almost. Stay here in New York or stay in this life? Stay.

"How did you know I was here?" I ask Jacquelyn, my brow still furrowed.

"This is your hotel. It seemed as obvious a choice as any." Jacquelyn smiles.

My mind grows a little foggy. All the objects around me grow distant even though I am here, in the moment. My glass seems out of reach. The girls on each side of me float like butterflies. I see money land on the bartop. The bartender waves at me as he fades into the distance.

Ding. I hear a dinging noise.

I am not in the bar anymore. I see lighted numbers in a small space as whispers float around my ears and butterfly kisses land on my neck. I feel like I'm floating upward.

Ding. There it is again.

I close my eyes to steady myself, only for a moment. I need to stay in this moment—keep a hold of myself. All I can think is that I drank something more than a couple of whiskeys and a pill. I clench my eyelids shut hard. I need to push it all away from my eyes. Push it down and flush it out somehow.

The sun beats down on me, reflecting off the white sands. I watch the sea as the waves silently and softly crash onto the shore, licking my toes. It sends a shiver up my legs. It relaxes me with each wave that caresses my feet.

I try to look at the endless beach around me. There is nothing but sand and ocean water. No other people around. No other sights. Just the endless white sands, gentle waves, and burning sun overhead. I am okay with this. The solitude is nice. I haven't had such time to myself in decades. I'm not sure if I've ever had this sort of alone time, time for just me and no worries about others. About the . . . whatever it was I was working on that was so crucial. All me and no one else. No one to set expectations on whatever it is they expect from me.

The tingling works its way up my leg. It tickles but also feels exciting, a feeling out of place where I am. I look down to see a hermit crab crawling on the inside of my thigh. I try to wipe it away, but I can't move. My arms won't move. I see them next to me, lying there like two lifeless flesh logs. Useless. It doesn't matter. The hermit crab is gone. But the tickling is still there. The feeling that something is crawling farther up my thigh, stopping at my manhood.

I am enjoying the thoughts that wade through my mind: feelings I can't place; ideas that I know are there but don't make sense; thoughts that are nothing more than lumps of clay waiting to take shape. The pieces know what shape they will end up taking, and that I am the one to shape them. I, however, do not comprehend what the clay thoughts want to be sculpted into. They are just there, in my mind. They are like I am—free of any responsibility, free of any burdens. Free from myself.

I feel no pain because this sensation tickles. Tickling isn't painful. Sure, it can be when someone gets a hold of you and doesn't stop while your breath starts to run short, and you can't stop laughing. That is a painful tickle, but this, this feels freeing. It reminds me of a playful tickle fight that ends in a deep, back-curling kiss leading to more.

I enjoy this moment. A moment when all worry slips away. A moment that seems as if it will go on forever. Just the sand and me getting licked by the waves of the ocean.

I wonder how I got here as I look around at the endless beach with nothing on its horizon. I try to recall why I can't move. Nothing comes to mind, just the peaceful lull of the waves and the warm, moist feeling of something wrapped around my special part.

I can't move.

Shit.

This feels too good to be true.

I am dreaming.

My eyes shoot wide open, knowing that what felt too good to be true is true. And the person making those feels in me is not Faith. The blinding light shooting through the window obscures her hair. I turn my head away from the light and see Jacquelyn sleeping soundly next to me.

Esther.

I shove her off and jump out of bed. I fumble for my pants that were luckily on the floor next to me.

I zip up and look to see her standing at the foot of the bed, wiping her smile dry.

"Good morning. I hope that was a fun way to wake up." Esther steps toward me.

I take a step away. "No, it wasn't."

She cocks her head.

"I mean it was, but it wasn't. I'm spoken for. You can't just start sucking off any man you think might enjoy it. There are boundaries. Clearly, something you struggle with," I try to clarify.

Jacquelyn starts to stir from the commotion.

"Come on, Finn. All the flirting last night. We hit it off pretty well. I mean, really," she shrugs, "what's a little blowie between friends?"

Something in Esther's words caught Jacquelyn's attention. She sits upright in the bed, still clothed from last night, a hopeful sign that nothing happened.

"I barely know your name. Calling us friends is stretching it," I shoot back. "And while I appreciate the gesture, you can't just suck someone's cock without their permission."

"What did you do to him?" Jacquelyn enters the conversation. The sleep that was left hovering over her has been pushed away by the force of my words.

Esther steps back, throwing her arms up. "Nothing that last night wasn't leading to. You promised me a good time, Jacquelyn. All I was doing was trying to make sure a good time was had."

Jacquelyn's face scrunches up tightly in disbelief of the words she just heard.

As the three of us stand our ground, waiting for Jacquelyn's words to form in her head, my phone rings. Of course, my phone rings. Nothing would add a little more tension to an otherwise already tense moment like a ring from Faith. And of course, the universe has responded with such a call.

"Good morning, love," I start the call with.

I try to wave my free arm to silence the commotion around me.

"You never called me last night," Faith says with a tinge of sadness and suspicion in her voice.

"Tell me you did not fucking mouth-rape him, Esther?!" Jacquelyn yells.

I don't know what I missed in the two sentences I had with Faith. I'm not sure why my wonderful and glorious arm wave of silence did not work. Hell, I really want to know what was said that caused Jacquelyn to shout like that while I am on the phone with Faith. I just hope Faith somehow didn't hear that.

"Finn! Tell me that what I just heard wasn't about you?!" Faith reprimands with a cold sternness in her voice.

"Jacquelyn, you promised he'd be down for all this!" Esther shouts back.

So, yes. Yes, Faith heard what Jacquelyn shouted. She knows that something happened.

"Yeah, and I was wrong," Jacquelyn snaps back. "That doesn't mean to just take what you want anyway!"

"Did you hear that, Faith? I was a good guy." I try to save face.

"Yeah, real good guy, Finn. Is that why you didn't call last night? You were too busy being a good guy?!" Faith's voice quickly rises in volume.

"I don't know." I start to respond. Probably not the best way to begin defending yourself. "I don't remember last night. I only had a couple drinks," I finish before shoving the rest of my foot in my mouth.

"You don't remember!" Faith yells. "I can't stress myself like this, Finn! I'm fucking pregnant with your child, but you have to run to New York for a record thing. Fine. 'It should only be a few days or so,' you tell me. Fine. Convenient you forgot to mention to me that you might embark on some all-night bender for one last hoorah before settling down into such a boring life with me, the mother of your child!"

Jacquelyn and Esther fade to the background. I know they are yelling back and forth right next to me, but all my mind can hear are Faith's words. I can see her black, curly hair whipping about at a hundred miles an hour as she yells. Her furrowed brow that bursts with anger yet looks so beautiful. I can picture it all. Perhaps I deserve her wrath. But in truth, I do not remember.

"You can't drug people just to get some party started! He isn't some lap dance club trick!" Jacquelyn's words resound in my ears, and I'm sure Faith's as well.

"Lap dance!? Finn, what the fuck happened last night?!" Faith demands.

"I didn't get a lap dance. Jacquelyn said I wasn't getting lap dances!" I plead.

"God damn it, Finn! We need to talk, and it's not something that we can do now. Just call me when you end your stripper session or whatever it is that's keeping you in New York this long," Faith finishes as she hangs up.

I know hanging up a cellphone is just a tap on the screen. Still, I swear I heard it bang against the base like old rotary phones. The sound and fury of hardened plastic slamming down over and over on those two little buttons that hopefully disconnected the call—I heard that in the digital tap on her screen.

But she said that we need to talk. Those words never predicate some great news. No one ever blurts out the ominous "We need to talk" and follows it up with something like, "Here's a new car I thought you might like." No, it's never good. But now I can concentrate on the morning BJ and why it happened.

"Hold on one second, ladies." I throw my hands out. "What the fuck did you say about drugs?"

Jacquelyn's lips tighten for a moment, knowing the revelation she has to enlighten unto me.

"She fucking drugged you! She thought it would make the night more fun," Jacquelyn says, with raised brows and scrunched lips, as she flings her wrist toward Esther.

I turn to Esther, who is standing there like some child who got caught putting a slice of turkey into the DVD player to see if something would happen. As innocent as the child might have been, her actions were anything but.

"Did you fucking drug me with GHB?" I ask, far more shocked than awed.

"And Rohypnol," Esther says, as if that is somehow better.

"Not any better, dumbass," Jacquelyn informs her.

"Why would you think that is okay? What, you listened to some love songs I wrote? Are you a deranged fan or something? I mean, deranged I get. Obviously. But seriously, you can't just go around drugging guys you want to sleep with." I grasp my head, trying to comprehend the intentions behind her actions.

"Okay, first of all, Jacquelyn said you'd be DTF. I was just adding a little spice," Esther tries to defend.

I swing around to Jacquelyn. "You said what?! You know what? It doesn't matter. Did you know she likes to drug her partners?"

Jacquelyn takes a deep breath and long exhale. "It's something we've done in the club if a big spender gets a little too handsy. It's not supposed to be a night-out-on-the-town trick to get laid by."

I shake my head in utter disbelief of the night's events.

"So, what the hell happened last night? What did we do?" I ask, still ignorant of what transpired.

"Nothing," Jacquelyn is quick to respond. "I wanted to. I thought it would be fun. I thought if Esther and I were able to do what I had hoped we'd be able to do, you would see that you didn't want to leave it all behind."

"I've done my share of drugs. Hell, I'm dealing with this shit still right now. But in all the years of doing dope and coke and whatever other narcotics passed my way, I have never been fucking drugged by a crazy-ass stripper!" I pause for a moment to quickly recall the two decades of foggy nights. "Nope! Not once!"

Esther steps forward. She begins to open her mouth to say something, but Jacquelyn holds up her finger to stop her from speaking.

"Leave, Esther. We'll talk later," Jacquelyn demands.

Esther hangs her head and heads out the door.

Jacquelyn turns to me. "Come on, Finn. We had something. It was fun. We had fun."

"What happened last night?" I stay on the subject.

"You were out of it. I figured it was too much alcohol or your pills or whatever. But you were out of it. You didn't want to do anything, much to my chagrin. So, we put you in bed, and we fell asleep," Jacquelyn pauses, looking for a reaction out of me.

I hear my phone ring again. I look down, hoping that Faith is calling back—even if just to yell some more. At least she would be speaking to me. But it's Viv. I let it ring to voicemail.

"Isn't this life the life you built? The life you wanted and worked for since you first picked up a guitar?" Jacquelyn continues over my ringing phone.

I stare at her, wondering what deranged person thinks that last night's events are anything like what musicians plan their lives for.

The phone rings again, and again it's Viv.

"Bad time, Viv," I greet her. "What do you need?"

"Contracts need your signature. You need to read over them and sign them. You fly out tonight. Come sign them before you leave," Viv demands in a most authoritative tone. She is no doubt taking well to her new role. A smile crosses my face.

"I have to go, Jacquelyn. Perhaps we'll talk later," I say as I turn to leave.

I open the door as she starts talking, "Do you really want to give up your whole life for Faith?"

I don't turn back. I pat down my pockets to make sure I have my wallet, phone, and hotel key. I shut the door behind me.

The events of the earlier day still play fresh in my mind. The contracts are signed, after making a few adjustments I hope the label finds agreeable. I find myself waiting for my airplane to take me back home. But the events replay in my mind over and over in their blurry remembrance. The words start forming in my head: something to write down; something to sort out my demons; something to summarize everything that is wrong with how Jacquelyn has come to view what could be our relationship. Or, at least, how I think she feels.

Vertical Fashions

(This is my love song to no one in particular)
You're choking on the words that your mouth
cannot form.
So you return to lay down, it's our relationship norm.
You preach of life's love and quick, dying passions.
Your words are flowing out in vertical fashions.

I Give As Good As I Get

So, we stand on our morals on rock-solid ground.
But our basis for love was, and is still, lying down.
We have never moved forward or found
piece of mind.
We've only looked back on this rockstar life of mine.

So, I scream, and you cry, and we will do it again,
Because we know you're scared to let it go
in the end.
So, I stay and I say that it might be all right,
But we know that it won't by the next evening's light.

To know that we both should have just walked away,
Because lying in bed is not where true love is made.
So, we say our goodbyes and hope it is not the
last time,
Cause we're knowing what is stirring inside both of
our minds.

You say I can't see you, but you're lying right there,
Writhing around and twirling your hair.
You say I can't see, but you are always right there,
Flat on your back with your legs in the air.

CHAPTER 8

We Gotta Get Outta This Place

My arrival back to The City Beautiful has come: Orlando, the place where adults regress to the innocence of childhood while the real world passes them by. The home of adult tantrums and a refusal to accept the truth of reality. The problem is that reality continues. The real-world moves along, and at some point, you must pull your gaze from the castle and face your life.

While I wait for my luggage at the baggage claim, I email the new lyrical set to Logan, asking her what she thinks and if it's something she can work with. Hopefully, this will be their first single. It's a little musical distraction before the reality of my life in Orlando hits me like a ton of bricks, but the real world awaits. I grab the handle to my luggage and yank it off the carousel.

As I open the door to the outside, I am greeted by the immense humidity and heat that imprisons the land we call Florida, a stark contrast to the comfortable interior of the airport. It is only a short wait for Faith to pull up to the curb in her car. Her eyes glare at me with a newfound hatred, my real-world problems all bundled up in the most beautiful and perplexing package a man could ever hope for. There is a strained smile on her face, to where any passerby who would happen to glance into the car and see it would know that behind it, words are waiting to lash out in anger. But here I am, back, home sweet home, and the real world awaits.

"Everything is fine just so you know," Faith says sans emotion, as I throw my luggage on the back seat.

I enter the passenger side and shut the door behind me.

"I'm glad you understand," I very naively respond.

"I was talking about the doctor's appointment you missed, jackass. Remember, the ones you said you wanted to start coming to." Faith keeps looking forward while she drives.

"I know. Slipped my mind. New York and all," I defend, trying to get so much as a glance out of her.

"Yeah, and all being some whore's mouth," she snaps, still looking forward.

"Let's not label those who choose the oral route of pleasure whores," I defend again with my mixed sense of currently displaced nobility.

"Yeah, stand up for your whore," she relentlessly continues.

"I didn't know what she was doing," I start to explain.

Faith interrupts with a glance that could make a pig squeal. "You didn't know what she was doing? You know, Finn, I don't know why I expected you to want to change, to want to leave it all behind for me. I mean, right after we broke up, you established the life for yourself that you wanted. Etched your name in the annals of rock history. Why would I ever think that I could be a part of that after all these years? Why would the inkling have ever crept in my mind to think that we could work?"

"I was drugged. I was sitting at the bar, enjoying a drink by myself, when this stranger started talking to me," I say, searching Faith's eyes for some sort of acknowledgment that this wasn't my fault. "Then, Jacquelyn shows up. The next thing I remember was being woken up from some dream by a blowie."

The pain starts to creep in. I notice it—a dull throbbing in my rib. Though it's nothing I can't ignore for the moment, it is just enough to make me take notice.

"That's the thing, Finn. Normal people don't do that to themselves. They don't put themselves in situations where they can be woken up by strangers doing suckie-suckie. I know you were drugged. And I should feel bad for you, and if you were any other person, I know I would. But you have spent the last almost twenty years surrounded by drugs, and you dare say this one time it wasn't your fault! How am I supposed to believe that, Finn? How am I supposed to believe that you weren't out just plastered and high and thought, 'one last romp before I turn the page.' Huh?"

I see a tear stream down her face. I know she and I have been through rough patches before, but there's something in this one that hits her hard. A realization that her glimmer of hope has died, the pregnancy, something I haven't seen yet. But it's there, defeat in her eyes that I need to win back. I need to understand so I can explain it to her.

The thump-thump of the pain grows a little harder. I wince though she doesn't notice. She can't even look at me right now. The pounding pain slowly waxing in my chest warns me that all is not well. I don't think I need that reminder, though. Faith is reminding me enough.

"Nothing happened." My words are quiet and calm.

"You said you don't remember," Faith responds in kind.

"Jacquelyn told me they tried. She said they wanted to, but I wouldn't, even in my drug-induced state." I keep searching for signs of love's life in her eyes.

"You are so powerful you withstood the date-rapey effects of GHB?" Faith skeptically says as she turns to me.

"Years of drug use may have its benefits," I joke. "She said nothing happened and with how mad Jacquelyn got when she found out what Esther did—"

Faith interrupts, "Who's Esther? Miss sucks-a-lot?"

I nod. "And when Jacquelyn found out, she was mad too. I promise nothing happened."

"I'm moving to Chicago," Faith utters.

My heart stops. The world around me crashes against a brick wall at 103 mph. The view in my sights cracks and crumbles right before my face smashes against it, draining all life from me. I don't want her to move. I don't want her to run. What happened wasn't my fault—for once, but I can't let this happen. I mean, I can't stop it, but I don't want her to leave. I spent too long hoping for a chance. Faith was the one who said no first because she had Ronnie. Things happened. Now she's pregnant, and I don't want it to end, especially not like this.

That reminder in my chest, that heaving pain that jabs at me with ill intent, is poking harder and harder. I can still wave it away, push it aside like an annoying child. (Wow! Like an annoying child? Some father I'll be!)

"I have to get outta here. This place is no good," Faith continues.

"It's not that bad," I counter.

She raises a brow in unsurprised shock. "Really? Forget the first night where you didn't even recognize me?"

"I may not have recognized you with your curly, jet-black hair and tattoos, but you did haunt my thoughts," I protest. "I hadn't seen you since your hair was straight and blonde-ish, and your skin uninked."

"That may be, but that night aside, what has this place been for me since you arrived? Blow jobs behind bushes, a parade of girls who I actually like as humans, which somehow makes it all worse. A dead boyfriend . . . fiancé . . . whatever. My sister getting married into the life that I never wanted for her. A life that I had to read about in magazines and the internet and listen to on the radio. And you at the center of the upheaval. It's too much, Finn," she finishes, while rubbing her eyes at the thought of her words.

"What about our baby?" I throw a Hail Mary.

"I'll be fine. I have friends back there. You don't have to give up this life of debauchery and gluttonous lust you've created. It's all yours," she says as I see the tears forming.

Tears are a good thing; it means she's angry. She still feels. If she feels, then there is hope.

This momentary glimpse of possible relief from the situation sets my pain slightly at ease, giving me a little more attention to give to Faith.

"I was on a job. I'm not saying what happened didn't suck. No pun intended. But I didn't play into it, and I didn't ask for it to happen. I'm here with you. It was just business up there. Contracts for Spear Fist and planting seeds with the labels for Logan Square." I stare forward as she drives.

"That's just it, Finn. It's not your fault. It's never your fault. You were drugged this time. We weren't together the others, so I couldn't hold any expectations. But I do! If you want something, you have to fight for it, Finn! You can't just sit and let the things around you happen without regard to how they might affect the thing you're fighting for. Ever think of that?!" Faith unloads. I can feel the weight lifting off her chest as she sighs with her full body.

Perhaps it's true. Maybe I didn't take others into account as my life happened. Perchance, I just lived in the moment and damned be whoever got caught in the crossfire. Maybe my inability to see outside of my own path has left ruins in my wake, but I can't look back and see what damage has (may or may not) been caused. I can only look forward. I'm sure if I want to look back, all I have to do is look to my left and see the tears in the eyes of the woman driving me home.

I let the heat of our words settle and watch the scenery around us for a few miles. I hope the silence settles my pains.

"How serious is this Chicago thing?" I calmly ask.

"I don't know. Fifty-fifty. Seventy-five percent. I got an offer. A good one at that. I just know that after all the years between us, then seeing you again. . . it was so much, Finn. I spent so long telling myself, convincing myself, I stopped loving you. Sometimes, I thought I never did. But I did, I do." Faith pauses to steady her words. "I can't spend the rest of my life reliving the past months in different cities and variations with random women. I need some little, tiny crumb of peace of mind."

"Then stay. Don't run to Chicago." I choose my words a little poorly.

"I need to see my sister. I need something stable, and you are not it, Finn. I need to know that you won't run away from me or screw things up. So, if I push you away first, then the only person I can blame is myself." Faith sighs, as if the clawing monkey has finally jumped off her back. How I hate being that monkey.

"But you can't guarantee that I won't mess up. You can't guarantee that you won't mess up. No one can. There are no definites in this life, not when it comes to that sort of thing. Asking for that is like when we used to ask for Jeanine to stop being annoying. She was who she was." I try to calm her.

"So what? You are just going to keep messing up and telling yourself, 'that's life'?" Faith waves her hand before turning on her signal.

"No. I will try to make it up to you. I will spend the rest of my life trying to make it up to you. I can promise that." I turn to her.

"You make it sound so easy," she huffs.

"I never said it would be easy. It will be hard and frustrating at times. You will want to kick and punch and cry. There will be times that we won't like each other as much as others. But those times will thin out and become less, and the good times will be more every day and less happenstance. And I think we owe it to ourselves, if not for each other, then at least for our child," I proclaim.

"I need my sister," she says, pulling into my parking spot.

"We'll take a road trip to NOLA. It's only ten hours. We'll make a mini-vacation out of it." I smile. "Vacay!"

Faith tries to hold back a smile that creeps across her lips, a smile that wants to wallow in the moment's pity but knows that some of my words were right. A smile that hopes the words of mine that were right were the hopeful words.

"It's not that simple for me." Faith laughs. "I have a job. I have appointments that I can't just walk away from on a whim. Those appointments are what pay my bills, put food in my belly. I'm not you, Finn. I can't just travel on a moment's notice," she rationalizes.

"There's like a week and a half before that show. Can't you make arrangements? Shift some things around. We'll only be gone for like three days," I rebuttal.

She purses her lips in thought. "New Orleans does sound fun. What if I can't get the time off? I need to talk about all this with my sis. This isn't some whim of a decision."

"Then quit. I'll take care of you. I have money," I say without thinking.

"I'm not some girl to be kept. I enjoy working. I actually enjoy the color, and the cut, and the asshole people who don't know that describing highlights as caramel is different with each person who asks. I enjoy the dumbasses who say they want a completely different cut, but don't want to lose any length or add layers. I do enjoy my job and all the frustration that comes with it," she defends.

"I didn't mean. . ." My fingers shoot to my chest.

There it is, back in full force. The pain that was subsiding has been slowly creeping back in. It sends shockwaves radiating throughout my torso, tearing through me like an angry alligator in a Florida gift shop, not to mention the migraine throbbing on my left side. I open my eyes wide to try and stretch it out of my head, blinking a few times. But to no avail. Damn, this hurts. I remember I ran out as I reach for my pills. Something I shall deal with later.

"So, what do we do?" I ask, though I'm not sure what I was referencing.

"I don't know. I'll figure it out." Faith turns my direction, her hand lingers on the keys. "This doesn't fix anything. It's not like one talk can magically fix us."

"No. I know. I wouldn't expect it to. One talk is just that. One talk." I let a little optimism seep out in my words.

"Exactly. One talk. I have a lot to think about. This is about more than just us now. I have to think about the little one. I have to think about my future and how it will impact whatever this is in me. I have to think about myself. My happiness. I have to think." Her hands slip off the ignition, leaving the car running.

I don't say anything. I just let the moment linger while her swirling thoughts come to a calm. I look at my place and think about the music behind those doors. I know as well as Faith that I have work to attend to. I have my future and our future to think about. I have work to do on so many levels. But I have her right now, and that's better than nothing.

Her eyes turn toward my home. "I'm not coming in. I'm not going to sleep with you. I'm not that easy. It's going to take more than one shower in a filthy hotel room to wash the mouth slut off your dong."

I laugh through my pain. "Completely under-stand. I wouldn't expect any less from you. My dong will be getting a few more washes once I'm through those doors."

I exit the passenger seat and grab my luggage from the back. Before closing the back seat door, I lean my head inside, arms holding the roof. "I love you, ya know."

A sad nod is given. "I know." She forces a smile. "Now go. I have to get going."

"Well, get got." I tap the roof of her car and shut the door.

I watch her drive away while rolling my luggage to my door. There's always a little part of me that thinks every time I see her leave will be the last. There's a bigger part of me that knows I only think that because if she were any wiser, it would be.

Love makes you do many a stupid thing. My phone dings, distracting me from my thoughts of Faith. Logan. A welcome distraction she is. She likes the lyrics and is mapping out the song. How I do like musicians that can work at a fast pace.

At least something with a positive outlook is in the works.

CHAPTER 9

I Don't Like the Drugs
(But the Drugs Like Me)

At work.

Two little words, but the succinctness says it all. When relationships begin, there are love letters and poems, songs, and (back in the day) mixtapes. Of course, that stuff changes. It doesn't necessarily die down; it just changes forms. The mixtapes become buying an album she'll enjoy or letting her choose the radio station on Pandora. The songs, poems, and love letters change form, too. Those become the little notes scribbled on a scrap piece of paper under a magnet on the fridge. It's a short scribble that lets the other person know what's going on and where they are, to ensure they know that they are okay and not missing or anything that would end up on a concrete slab in a *Criminal Minds* episode.

But these two little words—there is no love. There is no letting me know that everything is okay. I figured that she would have come back later that night, but I fell asleep. Perhaps she did come back while I slept but left. She could have found the fact that I was able to sleep a sign that I did not have any remorse for the events that occurred. Of course, I have remorse. I didn't want that girl, Esther, to do what she did. It's why I stopped it from happening. But Faith only sees the happening of the event itself. Perhaps she's frustrated that I am not angrier with the girl. The thing is, though, I can understand Esther's side. She was told I'd be DTF.

Any red-blooded, sexually awakened person would be happy if they were told they were about to meet a person of some fame who is down to fuck. She was just doing something that she thought would change my mind. Unwanted sexual advance? Sure, but unwanted advances happen. It wasn't violent. She didn't force herself upon me. She didn't hold me down. She simply made a move. Her intention, though misinformed by lousy intel, was not malicious or ill-rooted. Esther found a way to make her move that she thought I would appreciate. I think that's just part of the whole thing. Hell if I know; I could be wrong about it all. I could be the messed-up one. Faith might just be the more level-headed of us.

That would be the fine irony in it all. I wake up to some girl on my junk—a girl that I gave no permission and no sort of consent to—and Faith's mad at me, somehow rightly so. I can understand the anger on Faith's part. I can understand that without her having witnessed the events of the night before, she would think what she thinks. I'll just never comprehensively understand her inherent lack of trust in me.

Two little words: at work. Not even handwritten on a Post-It© note on the fridge. Just a text message. No love there at all. I can't help but wonder if there is something deeper bubbling below the surface. There's a part of me that wonders if Faith is in a sort of hellish torment, trapped in this life she has made for herself—knowing the feelings she had for me while still with Ronnie, and of course, how it all ended for her and him. The sadness in her eyes screams of a sort of guilt for what she has done and a desire to make things better. The last part of that I can be on board with. I think we, as human creatures, are always trying to move forward and better ourselves and our situations. We must push ever onward. However, that's what scares me, that she is pushing onward and leaving me behind—again.

But as pushing onward goes, I have work to do. If you can't be with the one you love, love the work you're with. A little more effort, and that would have been pithier, but you get the point.

I look over the lyrics that Logan has tweaked from what I sent. Minimal adjustments made can either be an excellent thing or a terrible thing. It either means that what I sent needed next to no work, or the artist is not as talented as I first thought. I'm really hoping that it's the first. I have interested labels and don't want to get them involved with a band that is less than what I make them out to be.

THE FRAGILE *Finn Fairlane*

A rhythm ticks on in my head as I read the words she is making her own. It actually sounds nice (at least the way I hear them). I let those sit because if she is making changes, that means music is being written. I'll touch that beast when I listen to it, which means onto the next set of lyrics.

This set I actually have music for; it's an old set that's always stuck with me. The sound of the guitar was initially designed for a noisy, distorted sound. Though, if I turn down the distortion and kick in some fuzz, making it more mid than low range, it will work for Logan Square. Plus, she eats up the lyrics of heartbreak.

The Old Way

Trapped inside this thing that I can't understand.
I have no way to grab the upper hand.
I keep weighing the options, but they only confuse.
It seems this is a battle that I'm going to lose.

Each day I look for reasons to stay inside.
Each day I find a reason to run and hide.
When I find a reason to live inside this,
confusion clears my mind, and it's then that I miss
The old way.

What I am inside is pulling me down.
Life's a circus, and I'm just a clown,
playing the one who enjoys the abuse.
If it ever stops, it's my life I will lose.
(I want to find a reason to like the abuse.)

I Don't Like The Drugs(but The Drugs Like Me)

Sometimes I look back at old sets, old songs that have been waiting for the right time to burst forth with life, and I question what the fuck was going through my mind back then. I have to ask myself what kind of person I was to stay in a situation that made me think those thoughts. I never did show those lyrics to Faith. I don't think she would have appreciated them then, and I don't think she would now. This then begs the question, "What is happening deep in my subconscious that I feel now is the time to bring life to that song?" Hell if I know. Could be the lack of communication while she bathes in her anger for me, or it could be my brain trying to tell me that this might end up the same as last time. Twenty years to repeat the same damn thing. It can't be that, though. Now we have a kid on the way, and that changes things, doesn't it?

I send the lyrics to Logan. Hopefully, she can find a good use for them. I have music if she needs it, anything to keep my mind off this pain in my chest. I'll just lay down for a nap.

The harsh light of day burns my eyes as it shines through the askew shades on my window. The sweet smell of pancakes and maple syrup hint in the background of my olfactory sense.

"Faith?" I call out, but she does not answer. "Babe, you here?" Still nothing.

I creep out of bed, my bones and joints cracking and popping in the early afternoon rising. Dressed in nothing but boxer shorts, I head to my kitchen to find a plate of pancakes topped with melted butter and syrup. The syrup has stopped running, and the butter that has since fully melted is starting to congeal again. Damn. It makes me wonder when she made these and how long I was out. The cakes are a bit cold, but nothing that thirty or so seconds in the microwave won't take care of.

As the microwave sounds out its triumphant ding of food cooked, I hear the click of Faith's heeled boots hit the floor.

"Jesus, you're just eating now?" Faith says with both shock and concern.

"Just woke up," I say, shoveling the food into my mouth.

"Well, get ready. We gotta leave in fifteen minutes." Faith's reply is curt.

"For?" I ask, oblivious to any plans.

"Doctor." She keeps it short and to the point.

The only solace I have that I might be wrong about her anger is her break from the distance she is putting up between us to make sure I am doing okay.

The pain has returned in full force, so a trip to my doctor is what I need, new prescriptions for new drugs to ease the pain.

Well, that was a crap visit. The doctor said, physically, I am fine. He couldn't determine a reason for me to still be in pain—but here I am still in pain long after it should have supposedly subsided. He said something about referred pain and psychosomatic symptoms, but it doesn't make sense to me. The pain is there, in my chest and radiating from that point of breakage. A pain that throbs. He told me it's all in my head. What the hell does he know?

Now Faith is on the psychosomatic wagon. She keeps reiterating the healing powers of positive thoughts (like I haven't tried those a thousand times before). I'd do anything to get this pain to stop, but it won't. She won't talk to me to let me explain the pain. I need something to dull it, if only for a moment, a split second of clear-mindedness. The god-damned over-the-counter pain relievers do about as much good as a non-alcoholic beer would be for keeping a buzz going—jack shit.

After my doctor visit, Faith went out with the girls from her salon, leaving me to my own devices. I pick up a guitar to try and take my mind off of the pain. The new-again music runs through my mind as I tweak it to make it Logan Square-worthy, a distraction that is quickly interrupted by the alert of my phone.

The solace I take in that dinging sound recently has become something for me, a drug in and of itself—if only a short-lived effect. At least it is something. Logan has been working with her band. Music, the all-consuming, ever-encouraging drug known as music, calls for me right now, a second round of homeopathic medicine to soothe my psychosomatically aching bones. (Damn, even I sound whiny to me right now.)

At least she likes the lyrics. Sure, she has made a few changes here and there, but the overall body of what I sent to her still reads very much the same. She just made them her own. I can dig that. She sends me an audio clip. The sound is crap, and for a band as punk-metal-whatever-label-fits-in-the-moment-here they are, she used an acoustic guitar to sample this for me. It comes across almost like a heavy march, something steady and regimented. I hear her reciting the lyrics in their timing while she is still working out the pitches. While there are no drums, bass, or any other instruments, I can hear the skank beat of the hi-hat and bass drum. I can feel where the bass line is pounding out its notes. When it all comes together, it shall be legendary. It's interesting to me that she sent me such a rough cut. I assume the excitement she feels needed to be released a little to someone who can appreciate it. I like appreciating and being appreciated.

For a split second, I feel the pain wash away. I feel good. The irony is that my momentarily alleviated pain gives me an idea.

[Finn: Hey, got any Vicodin? Dilaudid? Flexeril? Baclofen? Anything? Ribs are killing me.]

Send.

Maybe she knows someone who is holding. Possibly Logan will be my saving grace as I will be hers.

Almost no time passes before my ding sounds off.

[Logan: Slow down there, tweaker. Let me ask around. Jacquelyn's been supplying while on tour.]

I reply.

[Finn: But she's with you guys. Doesn't do me much good.]

Send.

I get a quick reply.

[Logan: She left NYC not long after you.]

I find it peculiar that Jacquelyn, who was following the bands up the East Coast, suddenly came back to Orlando shortly after I did. At first glance, that does sound awfully suspicious, but the world has more going on than my own happenings. I'm sure she had other reasons for coming back home. All I know is that right now, relief might be spelled J-A-C-Q-U-E-L-Y-N.

[Finn: Thanks. Great start to the song. Keep it up.]

Send.

I forgot to give her the new lyric set.

[Finn: Give me five, then take a look in your email. Working on something I think is right up your alley.]

All I get back is a smiling emoji, a great way to respond and end a conversation all in one little smiley face.

I switch my text message thread over to Jacquelyn. I know that if Faith were here with me, I would not be texting Jaquelyn. Faith is not here, so I can't think about the what-ifs and hypotheticals.

[Finn: Hey, Logan said you might have access to pain management.]

I hit send. Now, all I can do is hope she actually responds and isn't mad at me for what happened back in NYC. I know it wasn't my fault; it was all Esther. But sometimes people have a funny way of twisting situations to suit their needs and feelings.

[Jacquelyn: I might. Come over.]

That was quick and direct. I'm not sure if Jacquelyn knows I am actually looking to score some, or if my words were some sort of pill-popper's version of "Netflix & Chill." I'm not looking to just go over, pop some X, and do what the wild things do. Fuck it. I guess I have to go if I want the little helpers. That's the thing about my predicament; I'm not trying to put myself in bad situations or situations that can end poorly. I just need something, and she is apparently the only one who can help. For now, this is what I'll have to do until I can get the pain under control. (Isn't that what we all say?)

The drive to her house is ordinary—slightly cooler night air than during the day; some random accident with squad car lights warning oncoming drivers; the lingering smell of the day's earlier rain. But I think it is this ordinary mundaneness, the endless summer of Orlando, that has me thinking, if I never change my habits, if I am always doing the same thing over and over, I wonder how I will ever break myself of the patterns I know I need to abandon. If I can't leave those behind, I may be on the same track that leads me to be the leather-skinned, skinny man that staggers down the street midday in unwashed white shirts and torn jeans. Now I am wondering if this is the path I am on; that one day, my money will dry up, and I will be there, on the streets, with skin so tanned and leathery that when I die, some vagrant may make a perfectly good biker jacket out of me. There's a thought out of the serial killer's handbook.

I am curious as to how many of those staggering souls once started out as employees of the mouse cult. I think about how many were so underpaid, unable to cohabitate with others, that they lived out of their cars until that was no longer viable. The count-less souls lost to the dark underbelly of the cult of the mouse. There's a notion in my brain that everyone in the greater Orlando area is just a casualty of the mouse in one way or another.

I shouldn't be putting myself in these situations, situations that can end the way a good majority of mine have: random sex or strangers with candy that I partake in, or sometimes both. They are the endings that give others good pause to put up fences, walls, barriers, what-have-you of some sort to keep me at bay, at least until they realize I am harmless, or mean-ingless, to their lives. I guess if I want to change these behaviors about myself, I need to figure out why I do them, the root cause of it all. It could be as simple as being a Mr. Self-Destruct, or it might run much, much deeper than that. It might be that the reasons I self-destruct are the same as why I got into music in the first place. Solving one of those answers may solve both. I would not want to answer the reason why I became a musician. That would bring my world tumbling down. I'm starting to think that this drive to Jacquelyn's shouldn't have happened, that this wasn't my best idea of the day.

Too late. I pull up and can see the pool lights on the far side of Jacquelyn's house are turned on. They are not lighting up the block like some obscure inven-tion that pops out of the jacket of a small Asian boy, blinding his friends as they are making an escape from Italian mobsters. I just mean I can see the glare in the night sky peeking over the house. But if they are on, then she is in the pool.

Or was.

I put my car in park and turn off the ignition as she comes around the side of the house, wearing a bikini with a sarong wrapped around her waist in some feigned modesty. The glass of wine in each hand accompanied by the shit-eating grin on her face tells the world she is anything but.

"Come on, Finn." Jacquelyn grins. "Let's talk pain management."

With a quick pivot, she heads back to the pool, raising a glass that beckons me to follow. So, I abide. By the time I catch up to her, she is lowering herself into the heated waters of the hot tub, a glass of wine on either side of her. The mischievous look in her eye says this night is not going to be as fun for me as it will be for her.

"Come on in, Finn." She grabs a bottle of pills hiding behind her head.

As soon as I see the bottle, the pain in my ribs flares up like a dog running circles for treats.

"How much?" I ask, reaching for my wallet.

Jacquelyn shakes her head. "Silly man. Take off your clothes. Get in."

My mind is pulled back to my first time here—standing poolside, tripping over myself to be next to her perfect, naked body. Now though, the excitement is gone. All I want are the little pills.

"I'll tell you what, Finn. You take off your clothes, and I'll take off mine." She unties the top of her bikini and it slips off as the jets bubble around her. She sinks down in some 80s rock video attempt to lure me in.

The thing is a move like that would have gotten me in not too long ago for the exact reason she wants. Tonight, I must relent to her whims if I am to appease mine.

I remove my shoes, socks, pants, and shirt but leave my boxers on. I start to sink into the waters opposite from her. She hands me the untouched glass of wine.

I eye it suspiciously. "Esther's not around, is she?"

Jacquelyn lets out a hearty laugh. "You're safe. She's in New York."

I take a sip to show I trust her. Hopefully, it will move this along for me.

"So . . . now can I have the drugs?" I get straight to the point.

"Not yet. You owe me an explanation," Jacquelyn says. The flattening of eyebrows shift to a more serious tone.

I raise a brow, unsure of what explanation she needs. There could be so many.

"I'm in pain. I was in an accident, and the pain lingers." I sip my wine.

She shakes her head softly.

"We had something, Finn. We could have had more. You want the pills; I want to understand. I want to know what is not so special about me," she asks with a hint of desperation.

I try to find the answer, but I don't have one. If I did, I think I'd have been able to solve all my problems long, long ago.

Before I can answer, she puts up her hand. "No. You know what? What is so special about her that you would throw away the life you made, leave it all behind for her? Answer me that, and you can have the pills."

I look in her eyes, and we hold each other's stare. I see subtle desperation there. Not the daddy issue desperation that so many people think drives women to become strippers, exotic dancers, or whatever name you want to give them. I see a real lack of under-standing in her eyes. I see a need to discern if she is so un-special, or if Faith is just that special. Either way, Jacquelyn wants to know *why*.

I wish I could tell her. I can't because some things in life have no answer. Some things have no solid foundation. They exist because of the faith you have in them. Though, in the end, if we find the answers, there is the possibility the foundation crumbles beneath us. Either that, or it will hold firm and grow stronger. This is why I think so many people are afraid to question their own faith. They are scared of what would happen to them if they were left with no foundation.

"Cause I think you're scared, Finn." She trembles a little. "I think that you don't want to be happy with me. I think that you'd rather be unhappy with her because then you can continue to write your tormented lyrics and songs. You can continue to have fans—who have no idea who you really, truly are—shower you with empty adoration."

"That's not fair." I set my wine glass down.

"No? I think you are afraid that if you stay with me, you will lose that magic touch that makes music for the ages. I think that while pushing forty, you still have these high school notions of love and life. I think you are afraid that if you choose me, those fantasies that live in your head of how life should be will shatter, and you won't know what to do. You have no idea how to be happy," she cries, a mix of anger and sad realization.

"What do you want me to say? I don't have the answer you are looking for because I don't have any answer to give." I start to rise from the hot tub.

"I want you to say that you want me." She stands up too, her naked bosom exposed. "I want you to understand that you can have it all. The music, the touring, the girl who is into girls."

She stands naked—beautiful and crying. Nothing is between us as she lays it all out in her fury and anger. But I have nothing to offer her. I have no answer that will calm her pain like those little pills would have quelled mine. Now I leave, wet and without the pills. At least the dogs trying to burst out my chest for their opioid treats have gone back to sleep for the moment.

"I'm sorry I stopped by tonight. I shouldn't have come here," I say, zipping up my jeans that stick to my wet skin.

I walk back to my car, socks and shirt in hand, and wet feet in my shoes. As I get to my car, the sound of her crying has faded. I don't know if I can't hear her because I am too far away or that she has stopped crying. I know that I can't go back and check. I shouldn't have come here. I need to leave.

CHAPTER 10

Kings & Queens of the Underground

The time between my last night at Jacquelyn's and the New Orleans show have been a slow improvement. Faith has returned to speaking to me but still no leeway on giving me any pills. The pain, of course, flares at times, coming and going in waves. But my concern has been for Faith's well-being and for what will be our future child. As the reality of our situation slowly starts to sink in, I can see the sun setting on some aspects of my life. Not all of them, mind you, but some. I think it's an okay thing to see a setting sun. It means that the day is done, and that things are starting to calm down.

I think my time in Orlando has posed more questions and ponderings than answers, but if I had all the answers, I wouldn't have needed to move. If I knew all the reasons why to everything in my life, I don't think I would have had the success I had. I don't necessarily think success comes from knowing all the answers. I think it comes from continually striving to find them all, the unrelenting push forward to better oneself. To be able to figure out the answers to the riddles of my past will give me more of an ability to guide my future on this journey we call life. So, I push ever onward.

This push forward brings us to The Big Easy, Crescent City, that place known as New Orleans and to a sweet little venue called Tipitina's. What started as a local spot in 1977 has grown into a shrine for the man who helped make New Orleans what it is today, Professor Longhair. A sad note on my part that I never got the chance to meet such a great and honored musical artisan, but life has a funny way of putting the greats ahead of my time.

After stopping off for a quick check-in at Tipitina's, just to make sure everything is set for the evening show, we head over to my favorite stop in NOLA, Cafe Beignet on St. Peter Street. Everyone flocks to the other place, the beignet place for all, or beignet for the world, depending on your translation. There's nothing wrong with that place. It's just that, to me, Cafe Beignet is a little better. But I digress.

Upon walking in, Logan rushes me and grabs me in a most unexpected bear hug.

"You gotta hear the new shit, Finn! Fuckin' rocks!" Logan says with an energy high enough to light a city.

"I shall. Let us just grab some food real quick, then we'll detour to the recording studio." I grab a spot in line.

"Did Jacquelyn ever deliver on the goods?" Logan says, with the discretion of a howler monkey looking for a mate.

"What the fuck, Finn!?" Faith glares.

"Hey Faith!" Logan tries to recover her fumble. "How's the whole growing-a-baby thing going?" Logan waves her hands at the pregnancy belly, still yet to show.

Faith laughs a little. "Good. Just doin' its thing, I guess. How's the tour going?"

Logan's eyes grow three sizes in her excitement. "Fuckin' amazeballs! Great crowds, tons of album and merch sales! Time of my life!"

"So back to the man-child next to me, what goods were Jacquelyn supposed to deliver?"

Logan looks to me for an answer, but the cat is already out of the bag. No need to call it a duck.

Logan sees me wave her permission for the truth. "He was out of pills and needed something to take the edge off."

Faith puts up a hand for Logan to stop and turns to the garden area. She heads off while Logan and I wait for the food. Hopefully, she will calm down a bit.

"I didn't know she didn't know," Logan apologizes.

"It's cool. Just another tally mark as to why she thinks we will never work out," I relent.

"She'll get over it. You're a great guy, Finn." Logan tries to cheer me up.

"Don't do the whole pep-talk thing. It's not necessary," I tell Logan.

"Thank God. I felt weird." Logan laughs.

"You sounded weird." I laugh with her.

We grab our food and head out to where Faith grabbed a seat.

"Where's my sister?" Faith says to Logan.

"Hell if I know. She meeting us here?" Logan replies, scanning the crowd in case Jeanine is already here.

"Supposedly. I have some news," Faith says, joining in the scan.

"What news?" Jeanine says, as if summoned by Faith's words. "Sorry I'm late. Got stopped by like five different people wanting me to come into their strip club."

Faith says, gesturing to a chair. "Take a seat."

"Are you pregnant? Oh, wait. Yes." Jeanine laughs at her own joke while the rest of us shake our heads.

"Seriously, Jeanine." Faith's older sister sternness kicks in.

Jeanine's face falls flat. "What's goin' on, Faith?"

"I'm moving to Chicago." Faith lays it out for her sister.

"The fuck? When was this decided?" Jeanine says, shooting me an evil eye.

"Hey, I had nothing to do with wanting this move," I defend.

"No, he didn't. But he did solidify the decision," Faith continues.

"What? How the hell did I help make that a definite? We never talked," I ask, confused.

Faith turns to me. "That's the thing, Finn. You go to New York. Things happen. Things that weren't your fault."

"That's right. They weren't! You even acknowledged that," I interject.

"Then I have to find out your most recent indiscretion." Faith gives a condescending smile.

"Nothing happened while I was there," I defend.

Jeanine shakes her head and turns away from me. Logan scoots her chair closer, trying to get a better view of the eruption about to take place.

"Then why, Finn? Why were you at a girl's house who clearly wants you for herself?" Faith pleads.

"Like I said, I needed pills. I needed something to help dull the pain. You won't give me any. The doctors won't renew my prescriptions. I needed something," I tell her with sad desperation in my voice, akin to Lt. Dan whimpering for a treat.

Faith shakes her head and turns to her sister. "So, I am moving. I want to make sure that you'll be okay down here without me."

"I'll be fine, sis. I am a big girl now. Married and everything." Jeanine smiles.

"I know. I just want to make sure being so far from family won't make you sad or whatever." Faith searches for her words.

"Of course I'll be sad. You won't be near me. You'll be half the country away, living by yourself." Jeanine shoots me the evil eye again.

"Nothing's final yet," I interject. "We haven't talked about it fully."

I try to save face here and act like my words will have an impact now or on any future decisions Faith makes. The sad matter of fact is that Faith will do what she wants for herself and our unborn without any regard for me when she is mad with me. Always the worst of times with her. When we are on good terms, it's the best of times. There's never any in-between.

Faith turns to me. "Is there something about your life that I'm missing? Something about the tours, the days at a time in the recording studio I've been privy to read about in magazines throughout the years, the decadence and lack of a real home life that I'm missing here?"

I take a deep breath. It's not as simple an answer as Faith would like it to be. The fact of the matter is that in life and love, the answer is never as simple as anyone would like it to be. There's always so much more to any given situation than is seen at surface level. But now is not the time nor the place.

"I am moving with you" is all I say.

"So, you can find some other whore to buy pills from? Some other slut to wake you up with a morning suck session?" Faith's volume is rising in direct relation to her anger.

Jeanine interjects, "Morning suck session? I'd like to think that's an old story, but the tone of your voice says otherwise."

"Nothing more to it. Just that. Though, of course, he's not to blame," Faith tells her sister in a much quieter tone.

"I'm not. It wasn't my fault. We've moved on," I try to get back on track. "So, Jeanine, Faith needs to know that you don't feel like she is abandoning you down here when we move."

Jeanine grabs her sister's hand. "You need to live your life. Whatever the reason for moving to Chicago, you need to do what's best for you."

"Plus, now you'll have another reason to visit Chicago," Faith jokes.

"Much more often." Jeanine smiles.

"Cause whatever this thing is growing inside my uterus is going to need its Aunt Jeanine." Faith smiles.

"Of course." Jeanine looks down at her sister's stomach. "I'll be there as often as I can."

"Let's hear what you've got," I tell Logan through the microphone that feeds into the recording booth. Simple words they are, but they lead to many fantastic journeys. The number of times I have said those words throughout the years is countless and, in doing so, have been on as many musical adventures in those years as well. I never know if I will hear pleasant notes, rhythms, and beats that make my heart swell, or if disappointment will set in faster than greasy-spoon, roach-motel food poisoning. But those words I have said, and the show is about to begin.

Logan sits on a stool, guitar in hand, as the drummer taps off the four-count intro to set the beat. The bassist slides down the strings into the first beat of the song. The march-style beat that played out on the phone is now in full force. The keys resonate computer noise at twice the beats per minute of the song. It fills in the empty space of the sound without being overpowering. This journey is off to a brilliant start.

The first word chokes from Logan's throat. "Ch-ch-ch-chokin' on the words your mouth cannot form."

A smile crosses my face. I know technically speaking, Logan stuttered the first word, but it works in this musical setting. There's a touch of sarcasm that carries in her words, an emotion that takes the lyrical expedition down a dark alley, and I love it. The musical collaboration and cohesiveness that travels through my headphones and tickles my ears is what will be their first hit single. I am glad I was able to nudge things along for them, do what I do—create an environment in which musicians can grow and thrive. Now, for the tweaks. It's always tweaks and adjustments. Like they say, writing is rewriting, and the same is for music.

"I love it!" I shower them with words of encouragement as they finish the song. "The sarcastic direction you took it is wonderful."

"But?" Logan says back, tapping her feet against the stool as she flicks her right middle finger against her thumb repeatedly in a nervous tick.

"Always a but," I confirm, "but nothing bad."

"Bullshit," she fires back, already on the defensive. I see the raging vein begin pulsing to life in her forehead, a violent stream of blood and anger ready to burst forth, as if I am an enemy to slaughter.

I laugh into the mic. "Relax, no need to start fires. Keys need to come up a bit. They fill in the sound nicely but get lost once the song kicks into full gear. Mainly a note for the sound guy. The keys need to create the noise that will fill in the fuzz."

Logan cocks her head with wide eyes. "And?!"

"And nothing. I think you guys have a single here. Something with radio-play potential and the ability to launch you in a big way. The rest will come in how you handle yourself with any label reps," I say with softer tones, trying to calm her down.

"So, what? That's it? You find me at a fuckin' music store, give us a tour and some lyrics, and bam! Now we will get bigger?" Logan's tone is anything but believing the words exiting her mouth.

"No, it's the work all of you have put into your sound, the hours spent practicing, the image you have created, the years spent honing your skills. Then, a little extra added in by me. That's how it works sometimes," I say.

"No way," Logan argues back.

What I love about her is her skepticism. There's no need for it. There's no wool I am trying to pull over her eyes. No tricks up my sleeve. I am not some vanity label that waves promises of fame and fortune at a cost no one can reasonably afford. I am the money man and make it back on the return. And in return, they get theirs. But Logan has been beaten down for so long by life (and whatever else) that anything good is, and always will seem, too good to be true.

"That's it. You even said yourself that album and merch sales on this tour have been way up." I watch her nod. "The fans have been growing, and it is showing on the social media sites also." Again, I watch her nod. "So why not go with the flow? Enjoy this little wave as it turns into something bigger," I finish with a smile that tries to tug on the corner of her lips.

"But won't they all want something from us? Won't every label, every potential sponsor for a tour, all want something from us?" Logan tries to wrap her head around the mounting success of the tour.

"Of course. That's the nature of the business. But in that nature, you will get to create and play your music. And with me by your side, you will be able to create the music you want. Not some easily digestible and generic tune that the others would push for," I continue to assure her.

Hell, that is the whole reason I left New York in the first place and ended up in Orlando—to get away from the big labels that churned out music in laxative form, taken in one moment to be shit out and forgotten the next. It's the reason I was able to find Spear Fist and Logan Square. They are now my responsibilities to make sure they can grow on their own and can stand on their own two feet, confidently fighting their own battles without being metaphorically sucker-punched. While Spear Fist was already walking on their own two feet before me, they are finally ready to run. Logan Square is still crawling, but I will help them walk.

"So, now what?" she asks through the microphone, her voice earnest.

"Now, you guys play that song tonight at Tipitina's, one step at a time." I give them a simple answer because sometimes it is that simple.

I watch as they all look at each other with lingering disbelief in their eyes that slowly washes away as the realization of where they currently sit sets in. They are in a luxury recording studio in New Orleans, working on an album and a song that will be debuted tonight.

But this is the journey. Moments like this are why I became a musician in the first place, moments that seem so mundane without stepping back to get a view of the grand picture: the fact that she was a girl looking for a replacement, standing in a music store not too long ago, and is now touring the USA. She was angry over the fact the bandmate, someone she was supposed to rely on, count on, and trust in was more concerned about stickin' it in where it doesn't belong than the music. Now she is in New Orleans with an opportunity that may never have presented itself if it weren't for the happenstance of life. I am part of her happenstance, as she is part of mine. That is the journey or, at the very least, a small piece of it thus far.

We move ever onward into the night, which brings us to the long-anticipated Tipitina's, the big show of New Orleans. It's the last stop before Spear Fist and Logan Square head west for a short jaunt. The culmination of everything I have done for the bands has led us here. I say everything I have done as if the musicians themselves haven't been a slave to the music for years prior to my entrance into their lives. This night is the culmination of everything they have done to get themselves here. Perhaps my job is only to nudge them along when needed, nothing more. But now, at this moment, it doesn't matter. The stage is set, and Logan is on stage singing.

I am standing by the bar in a grey T-shirt, jeans, and a sports coat/blazer/suit jacket, whatever you wanna call it. My drink in my hand is keeping me company. The crowd is packed, but even in the elbow-room-only masses, I can see Jeanine and Faith talking. I am not sure this is the ideal location for Faith to have her heart-to-heart talk with her little sister, but it will have to do. Jeanine has married into the life that Faith avoided, a life that Faith had watched from the outside for years only to be dragged in now.

So, this is where they talk. I watch as the two of them exchange words while scanning the crowd (making sure I don't overhear them, no doubt). But I am a safe distance away, spying on them through parted heads and dancing bodies. What they say to each other is for their ears only. I am not interested in what they say. I can fathom a few guesses, and while none of them paint me in a good light, if any of the conversation is about me, it is for them. I am more intrigued by the mix of emotions I see on both of their faces. They both know that seeing each other every day will be a thing of the past, and that family get-to-gethers will be relegated to holidays and the occasional tour stop in town. But they both know that life heads in different directions at times. That, because they share a special bond, their paths may join again. They feel an emotional cupcake filled with an inner goo of hope and excitement, all on top of a bottom layer of love. But even in that weird metaphor of candied emotions, the sadness is what prevails. Like the icing on the cake, it is the first thing I see looking at them. The layers of their grief alone could make up another stupid cupcake comparison. But it is not for me to make. What I see is for me to absorb. Whether I am right or wrong about the sadness in their eyes and hidden joy creeping out of the corners of their mouths is not for me to find out. This moment is theirs, just as the moment a few feet away is Viv's.

I see Viv talking with a guy and a woman I have never seen. Judging by their wardrobe, they are the label I convinced to come down. Not a colossal name in the industry, but a start for Logan Square. Both of the reps are dressed in ripped jeans, not jeans that have ripped due to time and wear but those corporately ripped jeans. The jeans that try to say rebel, that try to say, "I march to the beat of my own drummer." They are jeans that try to stand up to the man and his conformist ways, but all they really scream is "I paid for someone else to do this to my jeans!" Even their shirts, fresh off the merch rack from some Hawt Tropics or Spenstars #metal-wannabe store, are decades behind the tour they boldly support. Damn corporate label guys.

On the other hand, it is these corporate label guys that are here because of me, the calls I make, and the ringing of my name in their ears. I just miss the smaller labels that get to wear shirts from actual tours, jeans whose holes have been worn into them from mosh pits and impromptu games of tackle football in some random field. Small label guys whose tattoos and long hair are earned, not gotten, and grown in some attempt to relate to the underground.

The woman has taken the lead over the guy, new face and new blood that seemingly takes the less aggressive approach. The female-to-female vibe could just be right. The guy may have said something that put Viv off, causing the other to step in. Maybe the woman is in charge. Hell, she could be in charge and he's just backup. Either way, I wonder about the other guy. Not my concern really, only an inquiring mind and all.

I watch as Viv's face is full of enthusiasm. I can see it in her movements. Her eyes are big as she talks about Logan Square and points to the various members on stage. While I am not sure why she would need to, I am sure she has a point. I see the label reps give courtesy nods and smiles, but I can tell they are losing interest. Luckily, so can Viv. She switches gears and stiffens her body a bit, not in a cowardly, retreating way, but in a way that exudes more authority. She has become a rock that won't let them walk away. This little gesture recaptures their attention. The female listens to Viv as she watches the stage with a hint of a smile across her face.

It's funny to me because labels rarely do this sort of thing anymore. With all the websites out there that have up-and-coming possibilities, they don't need to go to shows. They can sit back and click links, listen to submissions sent via whatever mail, and not leave their office. But for me, they come out. It's almost a way for the people in the industry to hold onto the good life, for the corporate guys to remember why they got into the business in the first place. It's a chance for them to live the life they wanted. They do it because, at the end of it all, it's the best way to see potential. Much like how movies are good on DVD in your home theater, but the experience is so much grander in a theater.

The guitars quiet down as Logan Square ends their song. This causes Viv's conversation to come to a halt while the reps listen to the group. The hushed tones, or what passes for hushed tones in a venue, break the concentration of Faith and Jeanine. Jeanine sees the reps next to Viv and sees something in both reps' eyes that cause her to whisper something to Faith.

"I hope you all're having a fuckin' great time tonight!" Logan follows with an uncontainable laugh.

The crowd cheers, which is a good sign for label interest.

"For most of you, this is all new music. But for those that know our stuff, this next song will be the first time we've played it." Logan looks out over the crowd.

The guitar kicks in. The marching beat of the bass drum follows. The rest of the band joins in, and the sound fills the venue. The crowd cheers as a small slam-style mosh pit forms near the front of the stage, only a few feet past Viv.

I watch as Jeanine watches Viv. The reps listen to the song and Viv. Jeanine starts to make her way to the three of them. I am not sure what Jeanine saw that I missed. Perhaps she heard something that signaled a need to move in. Or what Jeanine saw in their eyes was far more alarming to her than I noticed from way over here. It doesn't matter; she is there and has injected herself into the conversation with the reps. Jeanine gestures to the stage and points to Logan, as her hand gestures take on a life of their own. They are staccato in movement and sharp in their finish. She has captured the full attention of the reps. I don't think I have ever been prouder of someone who has spent so much of her life trying to annoy me.

As the song plays out, Jeanine's grandiose hand gestures are accompanied by the unconscious head bobs of the reps. They can't hide their enjoyment of the song as Jeanine looks like she is conducting an orchestra for the label.

Then I see it: a smile widens across all four of their faces. A release of tension overcomes Viv as Jeanine shakes the female's hand. I can see it in Viv; her shoulders drop and stomach arches out like she just ate a holiday dinner. Viv's smile now threatens to engulf her whole face as she shakes the rep's hand.

I make my way over to the affair. The short walk gives me a moment to pay attention to the tweaks they have made to the song from the studio earlier today. Logan and her bandmates listen well, and they adapt even better. The happenstance that was meeting Logan seems to have been more fate than anything.

All heads turn to me as I stop next to both sets of people, Jeanine and Viv on my left and the label on my right. I extend out my hand for quick handshakes.

"I see you've met Jeanine." I nod my head her way.

The female rep smiles. "Quite the firebrand you have, Mr. Fairlane."

"Finn. Mr. Fairlane is for when I die." I laugh.

The rep relaxes a bit.

"I trust that Logan Square is on the map for our next stop?" I look at both label reps.

The guy nods. "Once we get the contracts in order, we will send them over."

"Then enjoy the rest of the show," I wrap up the floor meeting. "Have a drink on me."

They both smile and part ways with us as I turn to Jeanine. "Nice recovery. What did you say that brought them back around?"

Jeanine leans in as if some big secret might otherwise be spilled. "I told them that different isn't bad. Change is different and can be what they are looking for. What they need."

I nod in agreement.

"Then," she adds, "I told them that the marketing potential for Logan Square and their talent is far higher than any pop-rock band that might be created in an office."

"Well done." I nod once more.

"Then, of course, I reminded them that you are on their team and Logan Square is on your label, which means less cost for them." She smiles.

I look her in the eyes, and while her words are about the band, her eyes scream Faith. Always the person on my mind and forever the person I default to, but I can't leave this behind. I can't put aside almost twenty years of my life for a four-year relationship I had in college. The songs I have written about Faith and the years spent yearning are the same as our relationship—in the past. Oh, but it's never that easy. Life is never that simple. Those best things worth having in life are worth fighting for. It's just a matter of figuring out which of those things are still worth having.

"Welcome aboard, Jeanine." I extend my hand.

"Don't make me regret this, Finn," she warns with a pointed smile.

I nod and take my leave. I need to find D.B. He has been absent as of late—since the tour and all. I need to hear what he thinks. I need the thoughts of someone who's on the same road as me, even if he is a little further back. I need the input of a guy—a male's perspective, a friend's honest and (almost) unbiased opinion on the matter.

I make it backstage to find D.B. talking to the label reps, except not the guys from just a few moments ago. These are the guys from NYC. Damn, I totally forgot I invited them. No matter now, though. I am here.

I overhear one of the guys say something about adding on a few tour dates. Not a bad idea if they are up for it, especially if it's on the label's dime.

"Will the tour still end on the West Coast?" I ask.

The rep shakes his head. "It'll end back on the East Coast. After they wrap up their last date in L.A., they'll stop off in Chicago again, then down to House Of Blues in Orlando."

"Sounds wonderful. Contracts all written?" I make deliberate eye contact with the rep.

He nods. "I'll just need D.B. to look them over and sign them. Tonight if he can." He pulls out a set from his briefcase and hands them to D.B.

I turn to D.B. "Got a few?"

He tosses his glances between me, the label, and the contracts. "We go on in a few. I wanna sign these." He holds up the contracts. "What's up?"

I see the look in his eyes. He's in show mode, and the contracts are the last thing he can deal with and still keep his head in the game. His look to me was a courtesy. The reaction he wants is not the reaction I want to give. I can respect his mindset because I've been there. I know how it is, so I put my concerns aside for the moment.

"It can wait." I hold out my hand. "Let me get a glance at those things before you sign."

He hands me the contracts. A quick skim has them twice in Chicago, then one in Denver and Vegas, two in L.A., one in Reno, Austin, and Chicago, then capping it off in Orlando all in under two weeks.

"Brutal but acceptable on my end. The jetlag is all on you guys. Ten shows in just under two weeks across the entire country." I raise a brow to D.B.

He nods and snickers. "Brutal for sure. It'll be great."

His smile fades and eyes get heavy. "Talk in Orlando?"

I give him a short upturn of my lips and nod. "Have a good show. See you soon."

Of course, I stay for the show and watch from the bar. But I don't just watch the band; I watch Faith and her sister. I watch the crowd. I see the world I know, the world I came from. I see how it is and possibly how the sun will set on it, the damn proverbial sunset. The funny thing in movies and books is when the old-timer passes on the torch, and the sun sets on his career, there is an unstated assumption that he is done and through. He is a horse put out to pasture, no longer useful in any way. A person who must now live out his golden years before becoming a burden to his loved ones and society. But that's the thing about setting suns. They rise soon after they go down. So, even if this is my setting sun, maybe the dawn will have something more significant.

CHAPTER II

Get The F*ck Out Of Here

Mine and Faith's return to Orlando was quiet. She slept most of the trip but was otherwise generally in a contemplative state of mind. There was a look in her eye that dared me to interrupt her thoughts, a look that silently screamed if I did challenge it, I would not end up anywhere close to well. I like that we returned home together, so I let her daring eyes rest. A battle for another day, perhaps. All I have to do is make it twelve days without blowing up my life. Twelve days till D.B. is back home and we can talk.

Day one.

Though we made it back to my place without any fights, casualties, or adverse happenings, I feel like we are in two different worlds. After an almost silent trip, she heads to my bedroom and lays down. No "goodnight" or words to have me join her. No pithy thoughts on her mood to break the tension that is slowly suffocating us. She just sleeps.

I still do not know what was said between her and her sister at the show. I try not to think about it, but my mind has to. Obsessing over the things in life that should be insignificant is what I do because, to me, nothing is ever that insignificant. Whatever was said has caused a sort of radio silence. I am done fighting with Faith. I do not want to cause any more stress, rile her up, or hear her yell. I want us to be okay, whatever that word means now. In a sense, I should enjoy the silence, relish in the fact she hasn't completely shunned me. Enjoy whatever time she has decided to give me before I blow it all up again, before she finally leaves me permanently.

But, in our silent thoughts, the truth wanders like a lost madman in a darkened alley. In my unwanted silence, my thoughts betray me and turn to Jacquelyn.

Our romance was short compared to most, but to others, it may have been a lifetime. But it was uncomplicated. It was new. Even in the end, there were still surprises; perhaps because even then, it was still fresh in many regards. Maybe I was drawn to Jacquelyn by her mysteriousness, a mysteriousness that hid who she was. A cloak of secrecy to hide her profession out of some intertwined sense of pride and shame. But she accepted me. She wanted me for who I was, not who she thought I could be or perhaps who I once was. With Faith, it is always so much more complicated. Complicated things attract us; it's the intrinsic human curiosity that drives our species to better ourselves and understand the world around us. The interest of the complication and the intrigue behind my eyes keeps pulling me to Faith, the eternal struggle between the Id and the Superego. Jacquelyn, on one side, is the comfortable side of things known and the peace of mind that comes with that. Faith, on the other side, is the one that knows it is where I belong if only I can figure out a way to get there without killing myself—metaphorically or literally.

All I know is that the longer she is silent, the more the pain slowly creeps back in. But as long as I am near her, even in her silence and sleep, the pain stays at bay. I must think. I must find a place to think and figure out my pain, my purpose in her life, and everything in between.

Letting you sleep. At George's Music. Love you.

The store is peaceful today, quiet and slow with only the employees wandering about. Well, the employees, me, and like one other guy. I let the thoughts wander through my mind while my guitar gently weeps. There is no budding musician that catches my eye. No talent that cries out my name. I just sit and strum, marinating in all the potential outcomes of any possible actions. But being away from it all seems to help calm my nerves. It instills me with a sense of serenity.

Looking outside, I see the sky is starting to darken. Either I've been in here much longer than I realize, or a scary storm is brewing. Any way it goes, I need to get back to my Faith.

I park my car and head inside as a flash of light illuminates the dim sky, followed by a roaring thunderclap overhead. It's only a matter of time until the storm hits. It's nature's way of telling me this is where I am meant to be at this moment. There's no leaving now.

The ominous weather outdoors is a stark contrast to what I walked into indoors. I smell cooking. If my nose is correct, I detect mushrooms and onions being sauteed and burgers whose aromas indicate my timing is perfect.

As I enter the kitchen, she greets me with a smile. "Dinner's just about ready." She flips the patties onto their buns and tops them each with the onion and mushroom mix. She carries the plates to the table.

I walk to the refrigerator. "Anything to drink?"

She nods her head. "A Coke, please."

I grab a can for each of us and join her.

"I wasn't sure when you'd be home, but I got hungry and thought you might like a burger as well," she says, taking a bite.

"I'll thank the storm for sending me back home." I smile. "Thank you for cooking."

"All the way back home, you never asked about Jeanine," Faith says in an unusually calm tone.

"I figured whatever you two talked about wasn't my business," I reply, swallowing a bite.

She sips her Coke, squinting her eyes at me. "She really has become a sister to be proud of."

I nod my head. "Quite the turnaround from back in the day."

"There's a tribe of monkeys, or apes, or some sort of primate somewhere," Faith starts on a seemingly off-topic tangent.

I raise a brow but stay silent.

"I read about it somewhere. An article. . . Facebook. . . some magazine. I can't remember. But I read about this troop, or congress, or whatever they're called, and how there was this male that joined their tribe after being ostracized from another," she continues.

"Okay?" I say, not really sure where this is going.

"At first, the male was aggressive and domineering. But the original males in the tribe wouldn't have any of it. They would defend against it, but not give in to the demands. Eventually, the new male calmed his aggressions and joined in the peaceful ways," Faith says, taking a quarter of her burger in one bite. She smiles as she chews. "These are really good."

"Yes, they are," I confirm.

"Then Jeanine asked if I knew the fable of the scorpion and the frog," she continues with a leading tone.

"Of course," I respond. "Scorpion needs a lift across a river. The frog agrees, and halfway across the scorpion stings the frog. Knowing they'll both die, the frog asks why."

"'It's in my nature' the scorpion responds," Faith finishes.

"So, you and Jeanine talked about Aesop?" I say, chugging down some Coke.

"She told me I can't be mad at who you were or who you are. Our past is our past, no matter how far back or recent. You didn't kill Ronnie. You didn't manipulate anything to be vicious or vindictive. The situations you inevitably find yourself in are not sought out by you, but rather, they seem to seek you out," she explains.

"Yes! Yes, they do," I start to defend.

She quickly throws up a hand and tightens her lips, a clear signal for me to shut the fuck up. So, I do.

"But, like the frog cannot be mad that the scorpion stung him, the frog could hope that the scorpion could learn from the monkeys," Faith wraps it up.

"Now I'm just confused," I admit. "The whole thing got a little convoluted."

She huffs in frustration. "I'm saying, hopefully, you can learn to see farther down the road to where your daily actions and the day's events might lead you back home and not to some rando girl's mouth around some random body part."

I smile and nod. "So, she stood up for me?"

"Hey, first time for everything, Finn." She takes down the last bite of her burger.

But this moment with Faith—the calm and quiet, the peaceful tranquility—it feels different. It feels almost calmly unsettling, the way the world quiets down right before a storm. It's like looking outside and seeing there's no wind yet. The sky might be darkening a bit, but it's calm. No signs of the approaching chaos until the wind kicks up without any lube to easy it in. Just full force, flinging loose furniture and ripping branches off trees. Now, all signs that things might be fine have disappeared—vanished from the surrounding landscape, replaced by the start of the show. The cosmic ballet played out by the wind, the rain, the lightning, and thunder leave no doubt that you thought calm was good.

Day two is rather mundane, just busy work for the bands, contracts, and all the boring stuff that comes along with the music industry. Faith is at the salon for the day, then heading out with her co-workers. This day is a day to ourselves.

Day three.

I decide to head back to Coffee Shop of Horrors. I haven't had their coffee in a while, and my body is jonesin' for it. There's a shortage of perfect coffee in the world, it'd be a pity to drink anything else. But my drive to the shop stops about a block short. They seem to have relocated since my first visit. This is a larger location, now full of baked goods and coffee-infused ice cream with nitro coffee on tap. They have really stepped up their game since I popped my cherry. Hell, they have a wall of board games for customers to play as well as hot sauce, art, books, pillows, bags, and other stuff for sale, all with the perfect horror/fantasy theme. Not to mention the giant television playing out some horror show. Time has definitely been kind to them.

I peruse the coffee selections for a moment when the owner steps out from the back.

"Been a while," the owner says.

"Sorry?" I didn't quite hear her.

"Haven't seen you since the hurricane," she rephrases.

"Good memory," I say.

"You're not easily forgotten," she quips. "You need help, let me know." And with that, she sits down in front of her computer. The location may have changed, but habits have not.

I grab a bag or two of almost every flavor because I am not sure when I'll be back in the area. Even so, it's not like it'll go bad. As I said, perfect coffee is hard to come by.

The owner laughs at me as I carry handful after handful of close to thirty bags of coffee in total to the counter, including four bags of a peanut butter roast.

"Can't decide or are you going somewhere?" she asks with a dry sense of humor in her tone.

Though it was meant as a joke, it hits me. I don't know. Neither. Both. All of the above. Some weird, unseen fourth option.

"A gift for that girl I was with. Plus, some for myself," I say.

"Still together, I take it," she keeps it short.

"Not sure we were ever apart," I ponder out loud.

Luckily, her life experience has taught her not to delve too deep with customers. She simply smiles and continues ringing me up. But her casual conversation has struck a nerve somewhere inside me. In all the years we were apart, she must have been thinking of me as much as I of her. Otherwise, that first night back outside that greasy burger joint in Old Town, she wouldn't have said anything. She would have just passed me by without so much as a peep or a whisper.

"If I don't make it back in, thank you for letting us stay as late as you did that night. Your kindness means a lot." I grab my many bags off the counter and slide them up my arm.

"No worries" is all she says. "You can always buy online. We ship."

I stop and look down at my armloads of hundreds of dollars in coffee. I just laugh in spite of myself. Something I could have figured out if I opened up a search engine before driving here. Well, ya live and ya learn.

"It's more fun this way," I joke at my own expense.

Day four is spent on the phone with the label from New Orleans. Sometimes, no matter what concessions I am willing to make to gain ground in the long run, things just don't pan out. I don't know if it was something said between Viv, Jeanine, and the label before I approached or if I said something. More than likely, it was nothing that was said. It was the simple inevitability of time. The label thought on their preliminary decision and decided against it. There was nothing I could say on the phone that would change if we were in person. In the end, the label felt that Logan Square wouldn't be a good fit.

Now, when I tell Logan, she will be crushed. It will feel like all her hopes, dreams, years of hard work, and sacrifice to the craft will have amounted to nothing, to being told her music isn't good enough. It will be my job to convince her otherwise. It will not be easy, and she will put up some sort of teenage resistance in the matter, as if I am fighting against her. I will be okay with that because getting her calm is my job. I will tell her there will be others. That I will find her the right fit and she will make something of herself and her band.

Day five arrives, and Faith again is working. I spend the day in my studio working on ideas for songs. It is a day of self-reflection and inner steadiness: a day to write and revise lyrics and music, and a day to think about whatever Finn needs to think about. (It's nice to know I still refer to myself in the third person.)

Dinner is just as pleasant. I decided to make a dish that is sure to please—grilled cheese and ham with oven-baked French fries covered in cheese, sauteed onions, and Thousand Island dressing, otherwise known as Animal Style for all you Hollywood burger joint peeps.

Day six.

The halfway mark and the point of no return (if this were a mission of miles) so to speak. I make a stop off at Park Ave CDs. I need to distract myself from the talk I desperately need and am being forced to wait for. The conversation with D.B. will give me much-needed insight into what I should do. The idea of my own label sounds fantastic. It really does. But this supposed move forward could be the proverbial sun setting on my touring days. It definitely looks like the sky is a few shades darker. Here's the problem with the sun setting metaphor: there's no clock. There's only the presumption the day is ending. No actual way to tell if the darkening sky is from the sun going down or storm clouds approaching.

I make my way to the store and finger through old vinyl records from when rock 'n roll ruled the world. Yeah, it still does in a sense, but it's changed so much. It is no longer the monster we once knew and loved. It has morphed and grown into something so different from what it once was. To look at the old and the current side by side, without what came between, the two would be unrecognizable. I look through old Rush albums, Talking Heads, Iron Maiden, The Animals, and so many more. I look at the inner sleeves (much to the chagrin of the employees) and stare at the pictures; the days of sitting in a studio—a my-hand-to-God, good, old fashioned analog studio. The mixing boards, reel to reels, microphones that by today's standards either sound like complete crap or have made a retro comeback. I stare at the look on each of their faces, the photos of them on stage or walking the back halls to the stage. The look in their eyes bares an excitement, an in-the-moment high and energy that never fades. Not just because it was captured in that one instance onto a photograph, but it never diminishes because the fire that burns inside of us never dies. Sure, it dwindles from time to time. The heat lessens like a bonfire in need of more wood, but unlike that bonfire, it never truly dies.

Maybe it's all just some nostalgic yearning for the early days. If I keep going this road, I may end up the guy who's holding onto his better years like the forty-five-year-old still reliving his glory days as a high school quarterback. Sure, my time was sweet. But perhaps my desire to create new music and new sweetness are blinding me to the best-of-times that are passing me by right now.

Whatever the reason for my thoughts, I am distracted by the sounding alert of a text message.

[Jacquelyn: Can we talk?]

Three little words. Three little words that will lead to so many more. I stand, pondering how to respond for far longer than I should. Anyone who stares at a phone this long without moving is clearly not in a proper state of mind. But here I stand, staring down onto the 3x5 screen, or however big a cellphone is, pondering those words. Frozen in the unknown of how I should answer, not because my words have escaped me but because I want to say yes and know I shouldn't.

Jacquelyn is my savior to stay in the life that I love. She doesn't judge me by my past and still wants to be a part of my future, a girl who never did get a fair chance to state her case while being told a verdict she didn't agree with, and rightly so. Life options aside, I enjoyed my time with her. She made me feel like the man I always wanted to be. She made me feel special. How fuckin' cheesy. A grown-ass man, with money in the bank, fame (fading or otherwise), and a history all his own wanting to feel like he's special to someone.

[Finn: Meet me at Old Town.]

After checking out with my handful of Talking Heads and Rush vinyl and some CDs, I head on over. The traffic is surprisingly light for this time of day, and I arrive at Old Town in what could be record time.

Jacquelyn isn't here yet, so I wait in line to order a burger from that same greasy burger stand that started this whole Orlando experience and the reunion of Faith and me.

It's funny, time passes differently in Florida than it does up north. There's no snow or real changes of season to let you know that the world is spinning, that time keeps ever marching onward. There's only the daylight and the darkness. It is the darkness that is setting in, a cool breeze that blows, and the multi-lingual noise that drowns out all distractions around me. I know I've said it before, but there really is magic in the night air. It's something you miss if you don't stop and look around.

Everybody needs to take a few moments to look farther ahead than ten or twenty feet. To look outward in the further down close distance—to where the sound doesn't carry into your ears, where your ears stop listening to the sounds around you—where you can really see the beauty in what has become so familiar to you. Like visiting Vegas for the first time, you stop and take it all in. The lights of the strip and the casinos whispering your name are all so much that when you first arrive, you stop and try to comprehend the vastness that is Vegas. That is what everyone needs to do with their surroundings now and again. It is what I am doing while I wait. If only because you never know what might inspire you, what might be found lurking in the ethereal surroundings that gets missed by those glued to their phones or focused on the immediate.

As I continue to take it all in, eating my burger and fries under the fiberglass umbrella, I feel a pair of arms wrap around me. I know these arms. They have a distinctive embrace that a part of me misses.

"Hey you," Jacquelyn says, slipping her arms from around me and taking a seat.

I pull a relatively fresh burger from the bag sitting in front of me. "Thought you might be hungry."

"Thanks." She unwraps the burger.

"It was funny you texted when you did," I say.

"Why's that?" She chomps down on her burger.

"I was at the store where we first met," I say with a bit of reminiscence.

"Look, Finn," she tries to interrupt.

"It's funny." I don't let her speak yet. "This little hub of the peninsula. The Orlando area. Things happen here that I don't think can happen anywhere else. The rain we get. The weather. It messes with our heads. With how we think. Personally, I think it's why this state has such a big drug problem. But hell, I'm just a rocker. What do I know?"

"Finn!" She gets a little louder. She will demand the time to say what she wants. "Listen, I need you. There's something about what you do, who you are, that pulls me to you. A gravitational pull I can't escape. I can't stop thinking about the shows, the night in New York, the days spent at my place. I need you, Finn. And I think you need me, too."

Jacquelyn pulls out a bottle of pills from her pocket and places it on the table. Not exactly a subtle thing to do in a crowded area teaming with cops, but as I said, this place makes people act differently.

The pain that always lingers just beneath the surface starts to rise up. Like a starving dog that sees food, it hungers for it. It crawls toward it but still has to inspect it first to make sure that this won't be his last bite.

"Jacquelyn, you never got a fair chance," I begin.

"We've already talked about that. Discussed the you and the me. You still owe me an answer," Jacquelyn says, wrapping her hand around the pill bottle.

"I'm not sure I can properly give you an answer," I say. I try to look Jacquelyn in the eye but keep wandering to the bottle.

"Why not?! Did we not have fun? Were you not falling for me? It's easy, ya know, being on stage or at the club. The guys, they crawl all over me, fall at my feet, trying to get a piece. They throw money at me. Some even shower me with gifts to feed their illusion that we are in some sort of relationship or that we will be if they spend enough. Tell me that's not all I was to you?" she pleads. The tone in her voice is filled with quiet desperation calling out from behind her false bravado. "Tell me I was more than an illusioned girl vying for the attention of someone who was never going to make themselves available. Tell me that I mean something to you."

"I have never been with someone who didn't mean something, even if only for the moment. You mean so much more than just that. The ineffableness of the whole situation. Faith's pregnant," I start to say, but I stop. I know those aren't the words I am looking for even though they were spoken.

"Her having your kid doesn't tie you to her. It ties you to the kid. You don't have to make something that represents a relationship work because of a kid. We had something. We felt something. I still feel it, and I know you do too," she continues pleading.

"You're right. Having a child with her doesn't mean I need to make some vague semblance of a relationship happen. What I feel for you is . . . not relevant anymore." Not my most choice words for a delicate situation.

She pulls the bottle away and stands up. "Of course your feelings are relevant, you ass. People think it's easy, doing what I do. It is, in a sense, if you are physically fit. Spinning, dancing. Those are easy if you can already dance. The tableside service, the private sessions you have to fend off the drunkards who think that, just because they took you private, they can assault you. That's the hard part, but you get thick skin in my line. It comes with time. But this..." She waves her hand between the two of them. "...this right here... it hurts no matter how thick my skin. I'm trying to offer you a way to the life you never wanted to leave and the life that I'm made for."

She turns to walk away, leaving me with the remnants of the food. She takes a step and stops, turning back toward me. "When you finally figure out yourself, you'll look back and only see everything you missed. Everything that could have been will have moved on. You'll look back and realize everything you once loved has relegated you to a footnote."

"You don't mean that." My words creep out.

"I'm pissed, Finn. You are doing a big thing poorly." Her tone is quiet, sullen. The weight of her words sits heavy on her shoulders. Her head hangs a little.

"Can I get a couple of pills?" I throw out a Hail Mary.

She laughs, even though her mood is still grey. She shakes her head. "The audacity of your words earns you nothing. You still haven't answered."

She walks off and disappears into the evening crowds. I finish my food and head back home to Faith.

Six more days.

Days seven through eleven were surprisingly calm. Faith and I decided to visit old Downtown Disney on the eleventh day, a relaxing stroll through the shops and restaurants.

"I leave in a week," Faith says, with a hint that she still wants me to go with her. It's an answer I still have to give.

"I know. Your boxes are packed and stacked," I say, watching a couple of kids turn the wheel on a mock cannon. They pretend to shoot at some unseen enemy.

"I'm not going to let that answer ruin our day." Her passive anger creeps out.

She drops the subject and turns her attention to a hat store. Nothing but hats. We stop inside and window shop for a while. She does her best job modeling the various styles, most of which look great on her.

She doesn't want any, though. Nothing extra to pack up. No excess baggage. She says this to me, as if it was a metaphor veiled in wide-knit lace made from thread-weight yarn. It drives the point home.

I just need to sort out my head.

Day twelve.

Twelve days was the time between D.B. telling me we'll talk once he's back in Orlando and him returning home. Twelve days can go by in a flash. Other times, twelve days can seem like forever. I never thought he would make it back home. Not that anything adverse happened to him while he was on tour. No, that all went swimmingly. But twelve days of watching Faith slowly pack up her life down here, twelve days of helping Faith pack up her life down here puts things into perspective. It says that the end is coming. By helping her pack, I am pushing the inevitable end closer to the present than it was moments ago.

I guess now I have to choose the ending. Always the dilemma. The sun will set on some aspect of my life. In some way, a part of my life will forever change. I have to figure out which part and the why behind it. That's why I am sitting with D.B., double-decker cheesy tacos in hand, as we once again surround ourselves with the hot sauce bar and local art.

Here's the irony in my mind on this whole conversation we are about to partake—I am in no pain. Perhaps it is my body's way of telling me that everything is gonna be all right. Maybe the pain that has been dwelling inside me now has a place to go, that sitting here is someone opening the floodgates and giving my suffering a place to escape. Whatever the reason, I am glad it is subsiding.

"Here's a strange turn of events: Jacquelyn and I have been talking a lot lately," D.B. says, picking up his taco.

My hands stop lifting the chip to my mouth as my eyes lock on his face, searching for the words he just spoke to repeat themselves with clarification.

"Yeah," he says, as if I had responded with words. Maybe I did, and I didn't realize it. Perhaps he knows what I am thinking and thus his response. "She's been at a ton of the shows on this tour." He looks down at his food to take a large bite.

While he chews on his food, I chew on his words. There's a hesitation in his words—a world of silence he is not saying—he covers like he has been practicing this moment.

"She must be a big fan," I say.

"It started at the bachelor party." He swallows his food. "After you were . . . under, she was cut off. Didn't know what to do or if she should do anything. Not that there really was anything to do."

He stops talking and looks to me for permission to continue, as if I can stop him. But I know that his look isn't seeking permission to go on talking, but that he has a more profound confession. I know all too well this tale he has yet to tell.

"So, you and Jacquelyn talked while I was under. Became friends," I say as he nods in relief and confirmation.

I leave it at that. There's more to D.B.'s story, more he wants to get off his chest. But it doesn't matter. The things he wants to tell me are all just part of the life we live. This moving sea of twirling space dust that envelops us tells our story, whether we want it to or not. I know what he wants to say, so he doesn't need to say it.

"She's not your average woman, Finn," he says with a hint of a smile in the corner of his lips. "Don't be afraid that your guys' sex will become stale or moldy. Not all relationships burn out in the bedroom. Don't think that every day will be a honey-to-do list of chores. Or that you'll walk in on her riding the cabana boy's pool noodle."

D.B. says these words, but he doesn't speak to which woman he is talking about. Maybe that's his point. Perhaps D.B. is much more a Rhodes Scholar than I ever gave him credit for.

"Jacquelyn told me about your growing obsession with those round, little pills. She also told me the question that prevents her from giving any to you. Jacquelyn's a good girl. Stripper with a heart of gold, if there ever was such a thing," D.B. says with bright eyes. "I love you, man, and don't want to see you end up just another rock 'n roll statistic, found dead on a floor in some hotel room. Make a choice. At least you have one."

His last five words were hard for him to say. They came out through gritted teeth. Teeth clenched by my position to have either woman—both of whom want what they think is best for me. One of whom no longer has a significant other, as tragic as those circumstances were. And another woman who wants it all.

Maybe I'm missing the point. Maybe the choice isn't between the women, but that I can choose to not end up a statistic.

Either way, as he said, at least I have one.

CHAPTER 12

Once In A Lifetime

"**F**uck them!" Viv says, downing her Jack and Coke (mostly Jack). Though I guess to get to this moment, I need to explain the surroundings.

The final stop on the Spear Fist/Logan Square expanded North American Tour—House of Blues Orlando, a night to cap off what has been a majorly successful tour, not only for Spear Fist but for Logan Square as well. Hell, up to this point, it has been a helluva ride for Viv and Jeanine too. Jeanine's marriage seems to not only have survived the tour but strengthened their relationship without destroying the band, which was a point of significant concern for D.B., Vincent, and Neil at one time. Viv, also, seems to be thriving on her childhood dreams of a rock 'n roll life. She and Logan are still happy, though, at this given moment, frustration has her grounded in the reality of the lifestyle.

At the bar, located to the left side of the stage, Viv and Jeanine chug drinks, telling me their thoughts on the label from New Orleans, the label that was supposed to pick up Logan Square. The label that has decided they weren't quite the perfect fit I thought they were. I know all these things they are telling me, having heard them time and again from the current label and others in slight variations. To Jeanine and Viv, this is the first time in the history of music a label has backed out of a deal before signing the contracts. To Viv and Jeanine, this is the worst thing that could happen. To me, it's just another in a long list of bumps in the road, hurdles on the track, whatever. To them, it's a first. So, I must treat it like it is a first.

"Fuck those guys!" Viv turns to the bartender. "One more round!" She then turns back to me. "We were so close."

"Viv, there's a lot to this business that you are learning. But nothing ever comes easy. After they passed, what did you do to convince them they were wrong?" I ask, sipping my vodka and lime.

"What do you mean what did I do? Nothing. They passed." Viv tightens her stance and scrunches her face as she defends her words.

"Okay, a little bit of knowledge is about to drop. First, you're fine. Don't close off now. Don't drop out of the race because they did first." I pause to make sure she is still focused on my words. I watch as Viv and Jeanine soak in each and every word I say while sipping their drinks. "It's been twelve days. Send them an email or give them a call explaining why they are wrong. Why I, Finn Fairlane, said they are wrong."

"But wouldn't they want to hear these things from you?" Viv asks.

"You work for me; your words are from me. State your reasons with confidence. Tell them whatever you think will get them to take the hook." I watch Viv's facial expressions to make sure she is understanding.

Her lips slightly show a small smile as she nods. She understands.

"Now call them," I urge her.

I watch through the growing crowd of people, to the opposite end of the venue, as more concert-goers flow through the entrance. I see the familiar face of Jacquelyn stroll through the door, only for a brief second. Then she is lost to the swelling sea of people. Maybe I was wrong. Perchance it was not her. Just my imagination. I continue scanning the crowd for her, but she is lost.

"It's ringing," Viv says.

As she says her words, the sound of a nearby ringing phone screams beneath the music.

A finger taps Viv on the shoulder. It is one of the reps from New Orleans, though he is no longer dressed in the factory-torn jeans and reprint tour shirts. He is not on official business but dressed in jeans torn from the stress of time. He dons a shirt that has been to more concerts than most people in this building.

Viv's normal flesh tone is taking on a deep red hue as the anger and frustration grow in her face. Her breathing is more shallow and forced.

As I walk by her, sipping my drink, I whisper, "Just relax. You got this."

"I believe you are trying to call me?" the rep says.

"I didn't expect to see you here," Viv starts off with a steadier tone and pacing to her words.

"After the New Orleans show, I had one of their songs stuck in my head. I ended up picking up a CD to mull it over," the rep starts off. "There was something about your words." He turns to Jeanine. "And yours, that made me think my colleague and I had it wrong."

Viv takes a chest-swelling deep breath and holds it while she chews her words. "You need Logan Square. They may have been the opening act on this tour, but their performance on stage and merch sales have been anything but opening act."

The rep nods his head in agreement.

I continue watching as Viv settles into a comfort level that allows her the confidence to reel this guy in. He continues to nod with each of her words. I smile as I see my legacy grow. Never a bad thing, though my whimsy thoughts of a rock empire are interrupted by a buzzing on my phone. An email from Spear Fist's other label. I open it and read the body of the email but not the attached contracts.

I walk to Viv and whisper in her ear. She stops talking, and a smile crosses her face as she turns to me. "Are you serious?"

I nod and step away.

Her forced confidence from earlier has left, and genuine conviction, backed by a label that is willing to sign Logan Square, has given her all the backbone she needs to talk with this guy.

Jeanine steps in and joins the conversation. The rep tosses glances between the two women as they all have a friendly chat. After a while of talking and drinking, the rep extends a hand and shakes theirs.

I walk away as the three of them lean against the bar and order another round. Sometimes, the things in life that seem like a sure thing are a sure thing. But it doesn't mean it will come without effort, patience, or some frustration. Both those ladies fought passionately to keep that rep on their side. Sure, the music being stuck in his head helps; it is always about the music. Though, no matter how good the music might be on its own, it is still good to have someone fighting on your side to make sure the world sees how wonderful you are.

As I watch them all laugh and talk it up, I can't help but feel a little melancholy, a little weight sitting on my shoulders, slowing me down, a trudge in my step. I don't want this night to end. I don't want the butterflies in my stomach churning my insides and making my chest feel the my-heart-is-about-to-burst-out excitement to end. Not that I've never finished a tour before. It's not about that. Tours end; it's what they do. But this moment, this uniquely stellar moment where everything aligns is what I want to last forever. The end of a one-man machine known as Finn Fairlane and the start of Fairlane Records (or whatever off-the-cuff name I came up with in that meeting) is being solidified right now. Viv and Jeanine cementing the deal all because I showed Viv an email that Spear Fist's other label wanted Logan Square as well. Viv saw the opportunity and seized it. This moment is what it is all about, a stellar moment in time where everything is perfect. Perfection is not a state of being by any means. Nothing is perfect. But if we look hard enough at the hours, days, months, and years spent honing our craft, we can see perfect moments. Moments where all the stars align, and the universe has blessed us with a perfect moment. This is it.

On stage, Logan Square is finishing up their set and will walk back to the green room to be greeted by someone they have only met in quick handshake meetings. Now, they will be talking about contracts, tours, and much more.

There is an irony in this night that is not lost on me. The place that ends the tour, the building that finalizes my need to work for myself and on better things than corporate-produced pop hits, this town that I loved to loathe for that magical, talking rodent, has me standing in the belly of it all—House of Blues Orlando. This place has taken me back to my earlier years, a time when everything was so much simpler yet so much more complicated. It transports me back to a time when I knew everything, and nothing was going to stand in my way. This place, right here, takes away the jaded eyes of adulthood and transports me back with rose-colored glasses. Clichéd, perhaps, but it's why it was built. I know it's just a moment in time, but it feels so perfect. Nothing going wrong. Nothing being screwed up by good intentions with no fore-thought. No pain. No regrets. Just this moment. All in this place of childhood innocence that is washing away the misanthropy that adulthood inevitably brings.

So, the irony is that perhaps I am wrong. Maybe, just maybe that magical kingdom I have held such contempt for isn't the horrid, gilded place I preach that it is. Perhaps, that empire is doing what it is meant to do—take you away from the pressures around you so you can see clearly. So you can look at your world with fresh eyes and see exactly what it is you are looking at—the forest and the trees, if only for a moment.

This stellar moment of perfection will end, and I shall be okay with that. There is a truck in the lot loaded up with all of Faith's belongings, packed and ready to make the trek 1100 miles to the place where she and I first began—Chicago. Chicago is where she is meant to be. It is where a salon awaits.

A tap on my shoulder brings me out of my day-dream and crashing back down to reality. Faith needs to head out. She has to be settled into her new place and start the grand opening of the salon in two days. I told her she should have left yesterday, but she insisted on staying for the final show. I am not sure if it is some lingering suspicion or distrust that she still holds for me, or a need to be near her sister as long as possible to make sure that Jeanine will be all right once Faith leaves. But Faith stayed, and now she will be arriving in Chicago within a half-day of opening her salon. If Faith stayed the night, she wouldn't even make it on time. Now is the time she must leave, a forced end to all things.

We elbow our way through the crowd of people, gently pushing those aside too enthralled in the show to see us trying to pass. I hear my name being called out, my name drowning under the waters of the music. I look around for the source of my name, but I see no one. We continue walking toward the exit when I hear my name called again. As Faith passes through the no re-entry part of security, I see who is calling me—Jacquelyn. Her voice is distorted by the blaring music and the night of shouting at the stage. I stand outside with Faith as Jacquelyn approaches. The whole no re-entry thing doesn't apply to my friends or me, but the metaphor is not lost.

Faith stops to let her have this moment.

"You can't just leave, Finn," Jacquelyn says with a plea in her voice.

I can already feel the pain start to creep back in. The restlessness in my lower extremities starts to shift from one leg to the other. I see what is happening here. The two women I am torn between, representing the duality of my life, are standing on each side of me.

"She needs to head out," I say, gesturing to Faith.

Of course, my words were not perfect. They rarely are when I speak. But the words were spoken, and Faith heard them. I did not say "we need to head out." I didn't say "I am heading out." No. I stated that Faith needs to head out. And that is what Faith heard, a choice unconsciously made in my words. It will not be an "us" heading out, not a "together" event. Just her, heading out on the road to her new life back in Chicago and leaving me to the life I have made for myself.

Jacquelyn steps out past the security of the no re-entry. We step away from the crowds of people to a quieter location. As Jacquelyn finds a place to stand, I can't help but notice her head is framed by giant mouse ears whose silhouette is a neon-light on some distant storefront or billboard.

Jacquelyn's framing in those ears is everything the corporation wants, for adults to hold onto their innocence against the rising tide of all that tries to tear it away. But my naiveté is lost. It has been for decades, and no amount of time spent wearing mouse ears or frolicking in the magical kingdom will bring it back.

"So, you're not leaving, Finn?" Jacquelyn attempts to clarify.

I look back to Faith, who is framed by nothing. No mouse to make her look like an overgrown child. No magic lights surrounding her. Just a brick wall behind her and a stark realism that is her showing her baby belly. Her long, curly hair that disappears into the black of the night sky and the heaviness in her eyes that look to what the future might hold. It scares her, and you don't need to be a mind reader to see how she tries to hide the consuming fear behind timid smiles and squinting eyes.

"What do you want, Jacquelyn?" I ask. I figure a straightforward question is what's needed.

The lights that line the silhouette of her distant mouse ears flicker and brighten for a moment. "A reason, after everything we've been through. After everything. . . I deserve a reason."

"What is she talking about?" Faith interjects from the stark darkness of where she stands. The clouds clear their cover of the moon, and its light shines down on her.

I smile at Faith. Her anger toward me only exists because perhaps I do not communicate those things I feel do not need communicating. And it is those things that I keep to myself, those things I think don't need be said, that maybe should have been told. It is within those quiet thoughts we keep to ourselves that reveal the truth about who we are more than the things we say ever could.

"Jacquelyn asked what it was about you that was so special. She wants to know what it is about you that keeps me from being with her," I say, turning back to Jacquelyn.

"We could have something great, Finn," Jacquelyn starts before I can tell her. "We could have this life together. Something for the ages. Something that will be written about in songs for the whole world to sing. This life. . ." she looks to the House of Blues, ". . .this is what you made for yourself. This is the life you carved out for yourself in this world. Your own little slice of heaven. I want to be a part of that with you."

Jacquelyn says those words, but they are not what I hear. I hear the truth behind them. I listen to the words that Faith never spoke because she didn't feel the need to express them.

"You want to know why Faith will always be where my heart lies?" I ask Jacquelyn.

"Yes!" she says, sighing out all the air in her lungs.

"You want the life. You want what I have. The elements that make up the lifestyle of the moments I have lived. You don't need me to have those things. You need to find someone who has those things. The person that you could still be with even if they lost all those things. Faith has never cared about any of that. From before our first big break-up at that graduation party, she never cared about the lifestyle. She never cared about being famous or the consequences that came with it. She just wanted me, and I was too stupid to see that.

"But Jacquelyn, you, you have someone you've been talking with. Someone who met you at your most vulnerable and still had a look in his eye when he said your name while we ate hot sauce-covered tacos. A look that said you mean more to him than you could for me. But I guess, more than anything, Faith gave me the inspiration to be great. She gave me the passion to write the words I have left behind in song. She planted in me the ideas that drove me to end up where I did. If I stay with you, it wouldn't be fair to any of us. You would always have someone else on your mind, gnawing away at the could've and should've. I will always be thinking of Faith.

"Faith is the reason I am who I am. I am not leaving rock 'n roll behind. I am stepping further from the limelight and into a much more comfortable seat. There is no other woman I would rather watch a new sunrise with than her. I never needed a girl who would strive to give me everything. I need someone who pushes me to be a better version of myself."

"But we could have had something so beautiful," Jacquelyn cries in one last attempt.

"No. We couldn't have. But you can. You can have the life you want with someone much more suited to provide it to you," I gently finish. "I say sunrise because I am not done. I am not leaving behind a legacy. I am still making one. There is no end to my career and no end to what I do. Now, I shall do those things differently. A way in which I can be with the one I love."

I turn to Faith, who holds back tears. At this moment, I can't tell if they are tears of joy or anger, frustration, or fear. But she is smiling uncontrollably, and there isn't a sight in the world more beautiful than what I see standing before me now.

I turn back to Jacquelyn as she tosses me a bottle of pills. "Something to tide you over for the ride up to Chicago."

I look at the bottle and back to Jacquelyn.

"I told you, Finn," Jacquelyn continues. "When you tell me why, you get your pills."

I look to Faith. Her raised eyebrows, tight smile, and shaking head tells me that she understands she was wrong about me this time.

I look back at Jacquelyn and toss her the pills. "Thanks, but I'm good."

I toss Jacquelyn my all-access pass so she can get back into the show and see the man she has secretly been falling for.

Jacquelyn looks down at the pass. "So, you're just walking away from it all? From everything you've built down here?"

"I'm not walking away from it all. Just moving it to a new location. That's the joy of music. It's everywhere."

Faith and I make our way to the truck and start the engine. As I pull away from Disney Springs and onto the roads leading away from Orlando, my thoughts begin to wander. I start to think about what my life would have been like with Jacquelyn. More nights of debauchery and hedonism that I lived out the past couple of decades. More of the same that is the game of rock 'n roll. It would be a comfortable life, a life where the challenges are familiar and comfortable. A world where I stay exactly where I was when I moved down here. But Jacquelyn, much like everyone else, deserves happiness. She deserves to be with that someone who doesn't resent her or think less of her because of the things he never was able to do. I would. I would resent her for staying. D.B. holds no resentment.

Now, as I start our journey to where we began, I think back on the life I lead. I imagine the moments in between what Faith told me. The quiet moments that Faith keeps to herself for all those years between.

I think back to a moment we shared on her parent's patio back in college. We sat under the stars on a chilly fall night, just her and me. We spent the night looking up to the stars, imagining the possibilities of what life had in store. We shared our guesses and had a good laugh before making love under all the possibilities. There was an innocence in that night, a naivety that the mouse strives for us to hold onto for just a little longer. I think it's okay to do so. The world is a relentless place, so stay young as long as you can.

The possibilities—that is what life is all about. Of all the different scenarios we played out that night under the stars, not one of them was what actually transpired. Our young minds couldn't even conceive of what would actually manifest. Not one of those ended with us having a child, moving back to Chicago, and starting over. Sometimes life is like that.

That was years ago, when we were young and embraced the world with open arms. When we let things come what may and smile while being battered by life. A time before we closed our grip and held our fists ready to strike, to defend ourselves from those which we once embraced.

Whatever tomorrow holds for us, I do not know. I can only hope to again embrace the ideals we once held onto so dearly, ideals that made the world a better place, if only for a while.

BOOK CLUB QUESTIONS

1. What is the significance of the title? In what ways is Finn fragile?

2. This books deals with several themes: fame, addiction, the rock 'n roll lifestyle, inspiration, dreams. Which ideas stood out to you? How were those themes brought to life?

3. Finn Fairlane has definite opinions about the effects of the mouse on Orlando. What do you think of his assessments?

4. Jeanine and Gregg seem to have a healthy relationship despite the pressures of the industry. What does this say about the possibility of this life for Faith and Finn?

5. Finn's choices seem to boil down to two women who each represent a different future. What do Faith and Jacquelyn seem to promise? What are some alternatives to the futures they represent?

6. In the end, Finn chooses to go with Faith to Chicago. What do you think of his decision?

7. What do you think will happen to Finn and Faith in Chicago? Will they ride off happily into the sunset to raise their baby or will the same problems follow them to a new city?

8. Should Finn be willing to give up his life in the music industry to become the man Faith wants him to be? Why or why not?

9. This series showcases several strong women. What do you think of Viv, Logan, Jeanine, and the other supporting characters?

10. Finn Fairlane has starred in three books now. How has he changed from the Finn you met in book one (the one standing naked in a rainstorm) to the one who gets in the truck with Faith?

About The Author

Nick Savage is an award-winning and Amazon best-selling author. He lives in the greater Orlando, Florida, area with his wife and two cats. He is an avid video game nerd, artist, and musician.

Series by Nick Savage:

The Fairlane Series:
The Fairlane Incidents
The Fortunate Finn Fairlane
The Fragile Finn Fairlane

The Nation Series:
Us of Legendary Gods
So We Stay Hidden
The West Haven Undead

Other Works by Nick Savage:

World Whore, D

MORE BOOKS FROM 4 HORSEMEN PUBLICATIONS

ROMANCE

ANN SHEPPHIRD
The War Council

EMILY BUNNEY
All or Nothing
All the Way
All Night Long: Novella
All She Needs
Having it All
All at Once
All Together
All for Her

KT BOND
Back to Life
Back to Love
Back at Last

LYNN CHANTALE
The Baker's Touch
Blind Secrets
Broken Lens
Blind Fury

MANDY FATE
Love Me, Goaltender
Captain of My Heart

MIMI FRANCIS
Private Lives
Private Protection
Private Party
Run Away Home
The Professor

DISCOVER MORE AT 4HORSEMENPUBLICATIONS.COM